Antoine Laurain was born in Paris and is a journalist, antiques collector and award-winning author. His novels include *The President's Hat*, *The Red Notebook* and *French Rhapsody*.

Louise Rogers Lalaurie is a translator from the French, based between Toulouse, the Paris region and the UK. She co-translated *The President's Hat* and was shortlisted for the 2016 Best Translated Book Award.

D0062392

Praise for *French Rhapsody*:

'Beautifully written, superbly plotted and with a brilliant twist at the end'   *Daily Mail*

'The novel has Laurain's signature charm, but with the added edge of greater engagement with contemporary France'
Sunday Times

'Anyone who enjoyed Laurain's previous novels *The President's Hat* and *The Red Notebook* will doubtlessly enjoy this new romp'   *Portland Book Review*

'Witty, nostalgic – I was completely charmed'
Woman and Home

'This gem blends soft humour and sadness with the extraordinary'   *Sainsbury's Magazine*

'A tale of dashed dreams, lost love and rediscovered hope that is also an incisive state-of-the-nation snapshot'   *The Lady*

Praise for *The Red Notebook*:

'This is in equal parts an offbeat romance, detective story and a clarion call for metropolitans to look after their neighbours ... Reading *The Red Notebook* is a little like finding a gem among the bric-a-brac in a local *brocante*'　　　　*The Telegraph*

'Definitely a heartwarming tale'　　　*San Diego Book Review*

'Resist this novel if you can; it's the very quintessence of French romance'　　　　*The Times*

'Soaked in Parisian atmosphere, this lovely, clever, funny novel will have you rushing to the Eurostar post-haste ... A gem'　　　　*Daily Mail*

'An endearing love story written in beautifully poetic prose. It is an enthralling mystery about chasing the unknown, the nostalgia for what could have been, and most importantly, the persistence of curiosity'　　　*San Francisco Book Review*

Praise for *The President's Hat*:

'A hymn to *la vie Parisienne* ... enjoy it for its fabulistic narrative, and the way it teeters pleasantly on the edge of Gallic whimsy'
The Guardian

'Flawless ... a funny, clever, feel-good social satire with the page-turning quality of a great detective novel'
Rosie Goldsmith

'A fable of romance and redemption'
The Telegraph

'Part eccentric romance, part detective story ... this book makes perfect holiday reading'
The Lady

'Its gentle satirical humor reminded me of Jacques Tati's classic films, and, no, you don't have to know French politics to enjoy this novel'
Library Journal

Smoking Kills

Smoking Kills

ANTOINE LAURAIN

Translated from the French
by Louise Rogers Lalaurie

Gallic Books
London

This book is supported by the Institut français du Royaume-Uni
as part of the Burgess programme.
www.frenchbooknews.com

A Gallic Book

First published in France as *Fume et tue*
by Les Éditions Le Passage, 2008
Copyright © Les Éditions Le Passage, 2008
English translation copyright © Louise Rogers Lalaurie, 2018

First published in Great Britain in 2018 by Gallic Books,
59 Ebury Street, London, SW1W 0NZ

A CIP record for this book is available from the British Library
ISBN 978-1-910477-540

Typeset in Fournier MT by Palimpsest Book Production Ltd,
Falkirk, Stirlingshire
Printed in the UK by CPI (CR0 4TD)

Tobacco is the plant that converts thoughts into dreams.

Victor Hugo

Looking back over the somewhat dizzying landscape of my life, I would say that before the events that turned it upside down, I was an unremarkable man, bordering on the dull. I had a wife, a daughter, a profession in which I was respected, and my criminal record was a blank sheet. But then, I was the victim of an attempt to oust me at work, my wife left me, and I had four murders to my name. If I had to sum up my unusual trajectory in one sentence, I would say 'it was all the fault of the cigarettes'.

It was in 2007 that the heinous law took effect. The law that drove smokers to congregate outside office buildings in courtyards where smoking was soon also banned. Janitors and office cleaners quickly made it known that the sudden increase in their workload, from all the extra cigarette butts, would rapidly become unmanageable without a consequent re-evaluation of the fruits of their labour. Businesses ignored their demands and smokers were thrown out onto the street.

'These heinous laws will have everyone doing it in the street.' I had suggested this startling phrase to my lawyer, with a subtle nod to Marthe Richard's law of April 1946 that ordered – with not a trace of irony – the closing of the *maisons closes*: luxurious, legal brothels across France, where champagne and other delights had been liberally dispensed for decades. Proprietors and madams suffered the torments of nervous depression, previously known only to bourgeois ladies of leisure and their overworked husbands. As for the girls, they found themselves out on the street. Self-employed, until they fell into the clutches of merciless, often violent, pimps.

Our sweetest vices – stockings and suspenders, champagne, curls of cigar smoke, sexy girls, packets of twenty – have been thrown out onto the street with the rubbish, with the State in the role of sanitiser-in-chief. The dreams of our elected representatives are the nightmares of science fiction: a world where no one smokes and no one drinks, where the men are all thrusting executives with dazzling teeth and careers to match, and the women are all smiling, professionally fulfilled mothers of 2.5 children. Sanctimonious laws for the good of one and all are building, brick by brick, a sad, uniform world that reeks of bleach.

My lawyer had been unconvinced by my reasoning, and even less about using it himself. Obviously, he would cite my nicotine dependency, but without making too much of it. I wasn't in trouble for having smoked in a public place – it was 'a little more serious than that, Monsieur Valantine'.

There are various ways to embark on a criminal career. The first is to discover you have a calling. Serial killers are an excellent example: from an early age they feel different and experience strong animosity to the world around them, coupled with a highly questionable determination to shape it to their own ends. Psychopathic, schizophrenic, paranoiac: medical terminology abounds for those who choose to dispatch their neighbour, often with elaborately staged savagery. And yet, since they repeat the same type of crime over and over again, they are quickly identified and generally end up behind bars, where they keep their psychiatrists happy and, more recently, make novelists rich.

It's very important to distinguish the murderer, who is an occasional killer, from the assassin, who is a professional. The murderer may be the unhappy cheated-on husband who, on discovering his misfortune, seizes his hunting rifle or his lobster knife; if his career ends there, he will just be called a murderer. But the assassin makes a career of murder. The number of murders and the resulting criminal record determine his right to the title. A murderer could also be a bank robber who finds himself cornered by the forces of law and order, uses his weapon and kills two or three police officers. He's dangerous, but he's motivated by money, not by bloodlust. That said, the desire to grab someone else's cash regularly leads to violent misunderstandings with bank cashiers.

Where among these examples would I place myself? I'm a little of all of them. I progressed from an initial blunder to fully premeditated crimes.

At the beginning of his career, the smoker is generally intent on killing no one but himself. But forces beyond my control drove me to become a killer of others. And not through passive smoking. When it came to murder, I played an active role. A very active role.

The train of events that drove me first to disobey the eleventh commandment, 'Thou Shalt Not Smoke', followed by the sixth, 'Thou Shalt Not Kill', was set in motion one winter, that grey-white season, the colour of ashes and smoke, in my fiftieth year.

I was a hardened smoker with a forty-a-day habit, and I had exercised the royal prerogative of smoking in my office for fifteen years and more. The first blow came with the introduction of the law that banned smoking on business premises, other than in areas specially designated for the purpose. Initially, at HBC Consulting – Europe's biggest firm of headhunters – we chose to ignore the ruling. The department heads were untouchable: no one would dare ask Véronique Beauffancourt, Jean Gold or myself to extinguish what was, for us, an extension of our anatomy. We were smokers of power. Nothing could bring us down. But dare they did.

The French Revolution probably had its roots in some rustic inn, one afternoon, where a man with a bigger mouth than everyone else slammed his tankard of wine down on the table and hollered 'Death to the King!', to the applause of the small assembled company. The man's name, the names of the men who cheered him on, and the inn where the scene took place are long forgotten.

Precisely the same thing happened in business premises across France, in the early years of the new millennium. At HBC

Consulting, the rebellion was sparked in the canteen, where the feisty workers found their Saint-Just in the person of a highly attractive young blonde woman who was the talk of the company during the brief time she worked for us. This long-legged creature, who was about as friendly as the prison gates I would soon come to know, loathed cigarette smoke with a vengeance. Her beauty was matched only by her intolerance of our poison of choice. And yet my male colleagues, who had been in the habit of lunching in nearby cafés, had all made a hasty return to the canteen. Despite its sub-standard food and drab view over the rooftops of Paris, overheated in summer and freezing in winter, the HBC canteen had suddenly acquired the allure of a changing room backstage at a fashion show. None of the men paid the least attention to their food – indeed, many ate nothing at all – but all were mesmerised by the new arrival's figure.

'She's temping here. She's a model really,' whispered the frightful Jean Verider – Senior Headhunter for the marketing sector – at lunch one day.

'You've spoken to her?' I said.

Looking down at his grated-carrot salad, he flushed a deep red.

'No, Françoise in Human Resources told me.'

The girl's beauty was plain to see; and her loathing of all of us, with our grey suits and grey hair, was plain to see, too. Her loathing of us and her distaste for the canteen job she was forced to take while waiting for cover-girl fame were, I'm sure, the Molotov cocktail that blasted our smoking privileges.

Our exterminating angel managed to convince the refectory harpies that they were entirely within their rights to insist on the smoking ban at their place of work. One day, as we were all arriving for lunch, Véronique Beauffancourt asked for an ashtray

and was refused. The large woman dishing out the cooked vegetables and sliced meat pointed to a small sticker she had affixed
to the wall with her fat pudgy-fingered hands, an act which had
no doubt given her a pleasure not experienced since her wedding
night. A cigarette inside a red circle, the latter scored through
with an oblique line of the same colour. Véronique, who was
going through a divorce, declared it was a scandal, and was
immediately backed up by Jean Gold with his collector's Dunhill
pipe (Caviar Collection). It so happened that Gold had set his
sights on Véronique. For him, the incident was very timely. The
union it led to continues to this day, because they still write to
me, always with the same slightly irritating greeting: 'Poor dear
Fabrice, …'

I remember asking, that lunchtime, if this was some sort of
joke. And the fat lady replying that indeed it was not, it was the
law, and high time it was respected, or prosecutions would ensue.
We were left speechless at the woman's nerve. Immediately, a
committee was formed to work out how to fight back and a
direct appeal was made to Hubert Beauchamps-Charellier
himself. Stirred by the fury at the smokers' table, even Jean
Verider — who was extremely reserved as a rule — was moved
to speak, asking where the blonde canteen girl had gone, for she
was nowhere to be seen.

A small, thin, short-haired woman, whom we all suspected
of being a Trotskyist, at first pretended not to know who we
were talking about, the better to stoke the mounting exasperation
at our table. Jean Verider could bear it no longer.

'The blonde bombshell, who do you think?' he burst out.
'This place isn't exactly overrun with them as far as I can see!'

The woman glared at him.

'Oh, I suppose you mean Magalie.'

'That's the one,' Verider agreed.

6

'Magalie left yesterday at lunchtime. We organised a small farewell drinks for her.'

'And we weren't invited?' said Verider in a choked voice.

'Canteen staff don't fraternise with the office workers,' she retorted, and turned on her heel.

The girl had breezed in, sown the seeds of our destruction and then disappeared. In less than two weeks, she had won over the canteen harpies like a white missionary converting a tribe of savages. It was a magnificent performance that we headhunters would have done well to ponder. Some people have a strange power of domination over others: a magical gift, capable of opening a thousand doors, either to heaven or to hell. Beauty is often a factor. Not always, I admit: Hitler, who stirred multitudes by preaching the superiority of the Aryan race, was short, dark and ugly. But that's a different story.

'It's the law.'

Hubert Beauchamps-Charellier, the sixty-two-year-old founder of the business that bore his initials, had pronounced this while drawing on his Montecristo No. 1.

'Nothing I can do,' he went on; 'that's just how it is. Soon, it will be the norm. Look at me, puffing on my Havana cigar; I'm an outlaw. But I'm also the boss. I'm all alone in my office, and I can do as I please.'

'We all have offices of our own, too!' We had answered in unison, we three smokers, like children kept indoors at playtime by the teacher.

Hubert Beauchamps-Charellier gave a muddled account of laws, smoking bans and contraventions, which could end up costing him dearly and causing problems he neither wanted nor needed. Then he said he had an urgent call to make to a secretary of state. It was early afternoon. We returned to our respective offices and, ignoring the incident, continued to smoke. Benson & Hedges for me; Capstan tobacco in a Dunhill pipe for Gold; Vogue menthols for Véronique.

That evening, I told my wife what had happened. She also said that I'd have to get used to it, it was the law. As a non-smoker, far from sharing my dismay, she was actually a supporter of the putsch plotted by her kind. After a Martini Rosso each and (in my case) two cigarettes smoked in the sitting room, we headed out to the Paris Modern Art Museum for a private view: an exhibition entitled Inflammatory Art: Smoke and Flux.

'Is this an anti-smoking show?' I asked her.

'No, Fabrice,' she sighed. 'It's conceptual art. About the Fluxus group. I've explained it all before.'

My wife is editor-in-chief of *Moderna*, the iconic contemporary art review. An expert on three or four artists whose names I can never remember and the official archivist of a fourth, who has his own museum in America. I say 'my wife', because we are still married. I have stubbornly refused all her petitions for divorce since my incarceration, and continue to think of myself as the husband of the famous Sidonie Gravier.

Having no opinions whatsoever in common with the person whose life you share is a risky business. Even, I would say with hindsight, impossible. I have always, I admit, been impervious to contemporary art. After many years together, I would pay a heavy price for our aesthetic differences. One contemporary artist would suffer the consequences, too, and achieve greater fame dead than alive. He didn't even have to ask.

8

I must say something about my wife because, in spite of all that came between us, I loved her deeply. More than that, I admired her. We met at a private view at the Centre Pompidou. The event was organised for the upper echelons of a select handful of finance companies. Cocktails were served. One guest, head-hunted by HBC Consulting, had invited us along. Jean Gold, always at the forefront of modernity, and also a connoisseur of art, had just joined the firm and persuaded me and a few others to go with him. The name of the show escapes me now, but it filled an entire floor of the museum. Gold wandered among the exhibits, scrutinising each with interest while I tried to locate the buffet. In the throng I had lost the client who'd invited us and I went from one artwork to the next, wondering if they really deserved to be called art. Waiters in white jackets circulated amongst the chattering crowd with silver trays of champagne. I managed to grab two or three glasses and drained them. There was no one to clink glasses with – I had lost Gold now, too. I remember many guests going into raptures over a piece of rolled-up brown felt on a plinth. Years later, I discovered that this 'tapestry without tacks' was by an artist called Joseph Beuys, and extremely valuable. My troubles that evening started with those tacks. Beside me, an elderly woman peered at the piece of felt with an air of intense concentration.

'What do you make of this?' she asked.

I thought I detected a note of irony and replied that, personally,

I wouldn't give a handful of brass tacks for it. She glared and recoiled as if suddenly discovering I was dangerously radio-active. Never in my life had I provoked such derision. I drained my glass of champagne and tried to ignore her rudeness. Was I truly so uncultivated that I could not understand this sort of art? I felt like telling the old crone that my mother was an antiques dealer and my father an architect! Doubtless, she would have replied that with a pedigree like mine I ought to be ashamed. I moved along, wending my way between the studiously incomprehensible sculptures. Sheet metal, bronze, plastic, glass, everything looked as if it had been salvaged from a refuse tip and thrown together at the last minute. I envied these artists, churning out hoaxes with such aplomb, and living comfortably on the proceeds. The exhibition included a dustbin; I remember it clearly: an actual dustbin, full of actual rubbish.

'That's life,' said a man next to me, gravely.

I turned to look at him. He nodded at me.

'Yes. Unsurpassed, never bettered ...' he added.

If his argument was that rubbish bins were unsurpassable, I wasn't about to contradict him. I would gladly have sold our office bins for their weight in gold to these enthusiasts. On top of a column there was a computer circuit, to which the artist had fixed some washed-out peacock feathers probably dipped in bleach. The whole thing looked like nothing so much as a crumpled mess and gave off a rather unpleasant smell. I peered at the label: *Oedipus 64*. I was none the wiser. Further along, a series of cork panels had been tacked together in a strange, twisting form that rose like a column. *Rachel in August*. Had the artist dared show the portrait to his girlfriend? I gave up trying to make sense of it all and set off in search of a place to smoke. It was high time.

I crossed another room, emptier than the others and opening onto a terrace that overlooked the piazza below, with its huge white funnels. On the terrace, I took out my cigarettes and lit up at last. No, modern art was not for me, of that I was certain. Beside me, just outside the door to the terrace, some thoughtful soul had placed a free-standing ashtray, already piled with grey ash. I wasn't alone in taking a break out here. My thoughts wandered as my cigarette burned down. What would I say to Sophie, who cut my hair and who had been my lover for the past six months? Sophie had told me about the salon she dreamed of opening, the colleagues who would join her if she quit. It was a fine scheme, but thinking about it, I couldn't picture myself in Sophie's life. Not forever. Our liaison was just that – a liaison whose charm would dissolve the minute it became serious. I turned the situation over in my mind, tapping my cigarette into the free-standing ashtray at regular intervals. I could see no way out of this romantic entanglement, which was anything but romantic if the truth be told. My cigarette had burned down and I stubbed it out in the ashtray before pressing the knob in the middle with the flat of my hand. I liked these vintage designs: the top spun like a roulette wheel, sending everything down into the container below. A piercing shriek rang out. I turned quickly. Had a woman been stabbed? Or groped? Not at all. A blonde girl was staring at me, more horrified still than the old lady beside the roll of felt. Almost imperceptibly, her bottom lip trembled.

'Wha— What have you done?' she demanded, slowly.

She then repeated, shrieking so that everyone heard: 'What have you done?!'

I stared at her in complete incomprehension.

'I've just put my cigarette out,' I said, as dozens of pairs of eyes turned towards me.

'But, but …' she stammered, approaching the now empty free-standing ashtray. 'That's a Frekovitch. You must be crazy!'

She ran out of the room. I stared after her, then looked down at the ashtray. Frekovitch? Not a make I'd ever heard of. Unless … I took a step back. I hadn't noticed the two red ropes on gilt posts that protected the ashtray. I had thought the large mirror behind it was there for decoration. But, looking at it now, the arrangement seemed somehow deliberate. A work of art? A handful of people stared at me, frozen in horror. Others carried on with their conversations and paid me no attention at all. The young girl returned, accompanied by a dark-haired woman in a pale-grey suit. She had a sleek bob, blue eyes. And she was attractive. Very attractive. She walked right up to me and looked me in the eye.

'Sidonie Gravier. I'm the co-curator of this exhibition,' she said coldly.

Not wanting to seem rude, I shook her by the hand. Which disconcerted her somewhat.

'Fabrice Valantine, HBC Consulting.'

'He stubbed his cigarette out on the Frekovitch!' yelped her colleague.

'Did you really?' asked the brunette.

'Yes,' I replied. 'I'm so sorry, I mistook it for an ashtray. Well, it *is* an ashtray,' I ventured, in my defence.

The two stared at me in silence, as if I had just told them the Earth was flat, I could prove it, and the rest of humanity had been very much mistaken, from Galileo onwards.

'I'm really very sorry, I didn't see it was a work of art; I'll remove it right now,' I said, turning towards the ashtray, ready to open it and retrieve my cigarette butt.

'Don't touch a thing!' commanded Sidonie Gravier, furiously.

'This ashtray, as you put it, contains the *ashes* of the artist's sister. Its title is *Sister in Cosmos 2*. Look, that's what it says, right there!' She pointed to a label on the base.

Then she heaved a sigh, muttering that now they would have to sort through the ash.

'Help me!' she ordered. 'And you' – she addressed the blonde girl – 'take care of Jack Lang; make sure he doesn't head this way.' I watched her assistant disappear, enjoying myself thoroughly now.

Sidonie knelt down and spread the lavish programme for the evening on her lap, into which I tipped the contents of the ashtray. Under the gaze of the small crowd that had formed around us, we fished out the cigarette butt and tried to separate the pale ash ash from the darker remains of the artist's late sister. Finally, we repositioned the ashtray behind its red cordon and Sidonie arranged the contents as best she could, in a small mound, around the ebony push button. When the operation was complete, she sighed again and looked at me. Her vexation showed in the two charming dimples that had appeared on either side of her mouth.

'May I offer you a drink?' I asked.

'The drinks are all on the house, Monsieur Valentin.'

'Valantine. Fabrice Valantine. I'll get you one anyway,' I added, hailing a passing waiter carrying a loaded tray.

I took two glasses of champagne, handed one authoritatively to Sidonie and clinked.

She stared at me and a faint twinkle came into her blue eyes.

'And what do you do?'

'I smoke cigarettes in museums,' I said.

She smiled thinly and took a sip of champagne.

'What about you?' I asked.

'Well, as you can see, I run a funeral parlour for the sisters of contemporary artists.'

It was my turn to smile. The next day, I left Sophie and began my life with Sidonie. Some might say, smoke got in my eyes.

At the private view for Inflammatory Art – eighteen years after the incident at the Centre Pompidou, and for the hundredth or perhaps the two-hundredth time – I found myself wandering among utterly impenetrable artworks, with nothing to say about any of them. It was here that I first came across Damon Bricker, a young French artist, though his distinctly English pseudonym would have been better suited to the leader of a rock band. A newcomer on the contemporary art scene, he had made a name for himself thanks to his vile mania for setting fire to our furred and feathered friends: as the disciple of a mad British artist who specialised in formaldehyde and preserved entire cows sliced into pieces, this blond-haired poster boy cheerfully chargrilled his animal subjects, using his blowtorch like other artists use their brushes. His installation of a life-size charred and black-ened chicken house, complete with hens, cockerels and a fox, had caused a sensation at the previous year's FIAC art fair in Paris.

For Inflammatory Art, Bricker was showing ten glass domes containing a series of urban pigeons, all similarly charred and blackened.

'Why do you do that?' I asked him.

He gave me a strange look: clearly, the question had never crossed his mind.

'Why?' he murmured, looking me up and down. 'That is the question …'

To me, the sight of the carbonised pigeons, like a row of post-apocalyptic scarecrows, was deeply unpleasant.

'Don't you like pigeons?' I persisted.

He stared at me with the quizzical interest often reserved for the naive questions children ask.

'No, nothing against pigeons,' he declared. 'But then Damien Hirst didn't have anything against cows, either.'

He was referring to the complete cow carcass sliced through with a chainsaw and immersed in a series of aquariums at the Palazzo Grassi in Venice. My wife had dragged me along to the art foundation's opening there, and the walls of the Hotel Danieli are doubtless still ringing with the scenes of marital discord sparked by the comment I had left in the exhibition's visitors' book. 'Perfectly sickening.' With my signature, clearly legible underneath. Apparently, the anecdote had reached the ears of the Grand Carboniser himself, since he reminded me of it now.

'"Perfectly sickening!"' He spoke the words with a seductive smile. 'So you're the great contemporary art lover?'

'Ever have any trouble with the animal welfare people?' I retorted, anxious to avoid dwelling on the Venice incident.

'Not that I know of. Unless you're about to report me to the Paris Pigeon Fanciers' Association, Monsieur Valantine.'

'Well, there's an idea ...'

We eyed one another in suspicious silence.

'Ah, you've met!' cried Sidonie, coming up behind me. 'Your pigeons are extraordinary,' she told Bricker. 'Aren't they, Fabrice?'

'Extraordinary. A great artist,' I said, then turned and walked away.

My wife stayed chatting to Bricker while I wandered off through the museum. Alone in a room on the ground floor, I found myself drawn to the bookshop, closed at this hour. My eye fell on a book in the window with a photograph of a leading tobacco brand from the eighteenth century on the cover. I couldn't help thinking that wars and revolutions aside, past centuries were infinitely more civilised than our own in which we burned pigeons and sliced cows in half to be exhibited in museums. My phone rang in my pocket. My wife was looking for me, as we were joining friends for dinner.

There were five of us, and happily the Grand Carboniser was not with us. As we walked along the street, my wife attempted to set me straight. I shouldn't pass judgement on artists' works to their faces, she said. It wasn't done. I replied that every artist was open to criticism, by definition. They had a duty to play by the rules, it seemed to me.

'They're highly sensitive creatures,' Sidonie insisted. 'With very thin skins.'

That didn't give them the right to blowtorch animals for pleasure, I replied, before letting it drop, as I had done so many times before. There's a point beyond which every discussion becomes tiresome, and I often reflected on the rules of my own profession: interviews of up to one hour and no more. Enough time to know whether the candidate is right for the job or not.

I tried to interest the group in a brasserie with a fine entrecôte béarnaise and a decent Brouilly, but to no avail: everyone was thinking of their figures and wanted something healthier. We wound up in one of those sterile Japanese restaurants that serve fillets of raw fish which look like French patisserie, all bright colours and asymmetric shapes, accompanied by delicate balls of rice. Nothing at all like a decent plate of food, to my mind, more like some kind of fish-flavoured dessert. As one of my British counterparts was fond of telling me, 'You're so French, Valantine!' Yes. He's right, I am profoundly French, with all the faults that implies. 'A Frenchman who likes an English cigarette!' the genial Londoner would laugh as I produced my packet of Benson & Hedges, though strange to say, he filled his pipe with that most French of tobaccos, Caporal Export.

Although I failed on the entrecôte béarnaise, I had managed to ensure we sat in the smoking area of the sushi bar. Our party included Michel Vaucourt, the Avenue Matignon gallerist, and his wife. We smoked the same brand of cigarettes. After our raw salmon balls in soy sauce and several glasses of sake, it was time for coffee. The conversation had dwelt mostly on the upcoming FIAC, at which the bird-blaster would be guest of honour, with a top-secret new work. Even my wife had failed to get so much as a scrap of information out of him for her publication. After a while, people were polite enough to ask what I had been up to at work lately. I told them how we had recruited one of the best financial directors in the business for a rival company. I had been in charge of the whole delicate operation, which had enabled me to make some important new contacts in the major media groups, and ultimately to repeat the coup for one of the big names in advertising.

'It's an art in itself,' Michel Vaucourt was kind enough to say. He understood well enough that I had never fitted in within their artistic circle, a situation that weighed heavily on me.

By way of thanks for his amiable remark, which had been met with silent acquiescence by everyone else around the table, I proffered my packet of cigarettes, having first popped one out for him to take.

'We smoke the same brand, don't worry,' I said.

'I don't smoke anything any more,' smiled Michel Vaucourt, raising his hand in refusal.

I stared at him in disbelief. His wife took his arm with a simpering look.

'Michel hasn't smoked for two months now. And he has a secret!'

'A secret? I'm sure Fabrice would like to know what it is, wouldn't you, Fabrice? You're having some trouble with that at the moment ...' said my wife, in a meaningful tone.

I wanted to reply that no, I had no problem at all with 'that', and even less desire to know Michel's secret, which he could kindly keep to himself, vile traitor that he was.

'This morning they announced a ban on smoking in Fabrice's canteen,' Sidonie continued.

'They're rather late in implementing that,' said Michel Vaucourt.

I couldn't believe it. Now that it was full steam ahead with the smoking ban, the rats were leaving the sinking ship. Vaucourt had joined the enemy. He was as bad as the barman – another smoker – at the Hôtel d'Aubusson, who, ever since his hotel had implemented the ban, had been vaunting the merits of his smoke-free workplace. 'I work better and I can breathe,' he told me, earnestly. This was a man who from time to time used to share a smoke with me at the bar. And he wasn't the first smoker I had seen rally to the opinion of the majority. Strange how people are apt to turn their coats once large-scale manoeuvres are under way. And especially in times of trouble. When France was liberated, Nazi collaborators were the first to rush to the Champs-Élysées and cheer General de Gaulle, whose broadcasts they had routinely ignored. Now the war on smoking was prompting the same calculated, cowardly behaviour, though it had to be said – and this was most surprising of all – it was, for the most part, genuine.

'Go on, Michel, what's your secret?' Catherine Dix, the fifth member of our party, wanted to know, even as she was lighting a Marlboro Red. 'I've been longing to give up for ages,' she confessed, exhaling a cloud of blue smoke.

Michel Vaucourt looked serious, then assumed the air of a man who knows his audience will laugh, but doesn't care. After a few seconds, during which everyone gave the appearance of waiting with bated breath for his pronouncement, he announced: 'Hypnosis.'

At that, I let out a kind of high-pitched chuckle, that took even me by surprise. My wife shot me a furious look.

'What's got into you, Fabrice? You should listen, not mock.'

Michel Vaucourt raised one hand in the manner of a Native American chief at a pipe ceremony who only wanted to make peace with the Palefaces.

'Fabrice has every right to be sceptical; I'd be the same in his position,' he said, with the assurance of those who have conquered something others are still wrestling with.

'I didn't believe it either,' he said, before explaining what it was that had made him see a hypnotist. It was a visit from a client, who had smoked three packets of Gitanes a day for over thirty years, then suddenly given up.

The renegade devotee of the soft blue packs had given him the address of a hypnotist that he'd been given by someone else. They were like an underground cult, passing the name of their guru around.

Vaucourt stopped speaking and drank a glass of water while the table sat in silence.

'You'll never keep it up, Michel,' I goaded him.

'What makes you say that?' asked my wife, instantly.

'It's only been two months since Michel gave up. Believe me, it takes longer than that to be sure you can stick at it.'

'How would you know? You've never stopped for more than

20

a week,' countered Sidonie, 'and I was the one who went out and bought you an entire carton of cigarettes, you were so unbearable! Yes, it was me!'

She looked round the table. 'You have no idea what Fabrice is like without his nicotine fix,' she added.

'Perhaps our friends aren't interested in the intimate details of our life,' I said, trying to wriggle out of the ambush.

'You aren't the only one,' said Michel Vaucourt's wife quickly. 'I went down to the café on the corner more than once to get a packet for him; he was dreadful!'

Too late: I could not stop the smoking-related memory mill from turning. In these colourful anecdotes, I was, of course, always cast in the role of villain. My wife was a saint, suffering the tyranny of a smoker, a kind of impossible house-dragon blasting everything in his path: curtains, velvet sofa covers, cushions, carpets, and not forgetting the colour of the net curtains – the water in the washing machine was completely yellow!

'Yes, yes!' chorused Michel Vaucourt's wife, excitedly. 'And the ceiling! Yellow! As for the tiles ...'

I tried to distract them by humming 'Yellow Submarine'.

'Haha, very funny,' said Sidonie.

I knew what was coming: dire health warnings. They arrived in volleys: I would have a heart attack in the middle of the street. I would suffer a brain haemorrhage. In either case, if I survived I would be left a vegetable. Or I would succumb to cancer. Hearing the litany of catastrophes, of which I was in any case perfectly aware, I found myself wondering whether people weren't wishing them upon me. Subconsciously. If one or the other struck, the people who had been warning me for so long would be proved right. The great 'I told you so' that covers whoever pronounces it in suspect glory. Wanting always to be right is one of the most exasperating of human traits: the pride that animals invariably lack. They are neither right nor wrong. They know nothing of these judgemental extremes. The observation of animals has played an important part in my life and I will return to it later. Animals are so much simpler than us, more rational. And they don't smoke.

I rolled with the punches and gave no reaction, but waited for the final knockout blow. I knew it by heart. Here it came:

'Emma's been smoking for a year now,' said Sidonie, in tragic accusatory tones.

I didn't reply but I looked her in the eye and sighed.

'Oh, don't look at me like that ...' she said, wearily.

'Your daughter smokes?' said Catherine Dix, who had just lit her second Marlboro.

'Yes ...' said Sidonie, quietly.

'That's not my fault,' I objected. 'There are young girls smoking outside every *lycée* in Paris and I didn't father them all!'

'It's not a joke!' said Sidonie.

'I'm not joking. It's just that her friends almost certainly have more to do with it than me.'

Obviously, no one was convinced. How could a father preach the evils of tobacco to his daughter with a cigarette in his hand? Emma, for her part, was taking full advantage of the situation, invariably answering her mother's comments with the words: 'I've watched Papa smoke all my life.' And so the problem was shifted expertly onto me, like a big gun readjusting its aim. All the reproaches aimed initially at Emma were turned on me. I was the man to blame, the Great Satan. I had transformed our adorable little girl into a small she-devil, addicted to cigarettes. Without wishing to absolve myself of any responsibility in the matter, I believe my daughter's smoking had far more to do with adolescence than with my cigarette butts in the sitting-room ashtrays. I wasn't the reason for her navel piercing, either, nor her dreadlocks and other eccentricities.

The conversation turned to our children, and their studies, and our fears for their future. But the seed was sown. The business with the hypnotist wouldn't end there. The psychological war being waged at the office had spread to my home. Two fronts. One man. I was bound to lose.

That night, Sidonie and I had a row. My scandalous desecration of the Frekovitch was brought up, of course. I decided to calm things with a visit to the charlatan practitioner. At least I could say I had tried and it hadn't worked. At least then I would be left in peace. Or so I believed at the time.

'What was the name of that wonder magician?' I asked.

My wife took out her diary, in which she had carefully inscribed a name, address and telephone number.

'Marco Di Caro,' she said.

So this is where my life as a smoker would end, here in this consulting room. I had gone to the address shown, on Rue Lamarck, and looked at my reflection in the brand-new shiny brass plate (*Marco Di Caro – Hypnosis*) before climbing the stairs to the sixth floor. Sixth floor, right-hand side. I pressed the bell. It made no sound. Then, a faint buzzing and the door opened. A card placed on a chest of drawers bore a small illustration of a hand, pointing to the waiting room. The walls were freshly painted, with no pictures. The room was furnished with a large sofa, two chairs and a coffee table spread with brochures and copies of *Libération*. The parquet floor shone in the late-afternoon sunshine. I settled into the comfortable green-velvet sofa. A coffee, ashtray and cigarette would have made it perfect.

A month had gone by since the dinner with Michel Vaucourt. I had been delighted to receive a bonus of thirty-six thousand euros for an exchange of rooks on the great chessboard of the business world. In our profession, we receive the equivalent of two months of our candidate's salary if the deal goes through, a fee designed to ensure we pursue the best deals right through to completion. I had taken my wife and daughter to the Jules Verne restaurant in the Eiffel Tower to celebrate. That evening, cognac in hand, gazing out over Paris, I had capitulated.

'I'll go and see Marco Di Caro,' I announced.

My wife placed her hand on mine, and we smiled at each other. I'd have done better to break both kneecaps on the Tower's stairs, but the restaurant is reached solely via its own private lift, so that possibility was denied me. Emma had jumped at the chance to strike a tobacco-related deal of her own: she would stop smoking if we allowed her to take a holiday in Barcelona with her boyfriend.

'And how will we know if you smoke when you get there?' I couldn't help asking.

Emma flushed scarlet: it was unbelievable that I could even think she'd break her promise. My wife sprang to her defence. Unable to face any more controversy, I agreed to sacrifice a percentage of my bonus to send my offspring on a holiday in the sun, in exchange for her dubious assurance. With a firm hand on the purse strings, for once, I had taken advantage of the situation, to negotiate the immediate and permanent removal of her navel piercing. This was granted as a peace token and duly deposited in a soap dish in the bathroom that very evening. The next day, I smuggled it out and threw it away for good. Claiming not to have touched it, I blamed the cleaning lady, who had just left and was unable to contradict me.

What on earth was I doing consulting a hypnotist?

'Ridiculous,' I muttered.

I should have tried Champix, the new drug that had replaced the more problematic Zyban. The latter was an antidepressant and I had forbidden myself from touching it. My workmate Jean Gold had tried Zyban a couple of years earlier in an effort to quit pipe-smoking, and the treatment had had some odd effects. He claimed he experienced the same dream every night, in which he found himself attending a conference in Dubai, where he was forced to share his hotel suite with Adolf Hitler. The dream began with him waking up to see the Führer's things placed on the bedroom chair, after which Gold followed the sound of running water coming from the bathroom. Pushing the door, he found Hitler in a foam bath, asking for toothpaste in German. Down in reception, the concierge would calmly explain that he couldn't possibly occupy the suite on his own and that he would have to share it with Hitler, who was a valued customer, polite, tidy, with a fine sense of humour. Furthermore, the Führer was perfectly happy with the arrangement.

'Then, a division of the Wehrmacht stormed into the lobby, dressed in fluorescent pink, and that's when I would wake up. You can see why I had to take up smoking again!' he told me, lighting his pipe.

He had written to the drug's manufacturer to tell them about its unwelcome side effect, but had received no reply.

I bent to look at a pile of pale-blue papers on the coffee table. At the top of the first page a heading in large letters read, 'WHY HYPNOSIS?' Marco Di Caro was pushing his sales pitch even here in the waiting room. Perhaps he was also hoping to convince the sceptics, of which I was certainly one. I skimmed the print-out, which recounted the history of hypnosis from the dawn of time to the present, through Ancient Rome and China. I skipped from one chapter heading to the next: 'Conquer Your Fear', 'The Mental Health Audit', 'The Keys to the Self' … On the last page, I found an impressive list of urges:

1. To drink
2. To take drugs
3. To bite your fingernails
4. To snack between meals

5. To wash (excessively)
6. To sleep (all the time)
7. To scratch
8. To smoke

...

Clearly, I was prone to urges. Right now I had an irresistible urge to light up, and wondered if by opening the window I could enjoy a quiet cigarette as I gazed out over the rooftops of Paris. Then all I would have to do would be to crush it under my heel, roll the last shreds of tobacco between my thumb and index finger and slip the butt into my jacket pocket. I had often resorted to this well-known tactic used by smokers with no ashtray to hand: you left no trace; all clues were removed from the scene. Like a hardened criminal, one might say.

My plan was aborted when the door opened. A very tall, well-built man with a beard stood there. I hadn't heard him approach.

'Monsieur Valantine ...'

I got to my feet and walked with him to his consulting room. It was much smaller than the waiting room – perhaps it had once been a child's bedroom – but it, too, had been freshly painted. There was a table, a black leather office chair, a purple velvet couch, and a second, smaller chair. Without a word, Marco Di Caro sat down behind the table and indicated that I should sit in the other chair.

'Who recommended me?' he asked.

'A friend.'

He nodded, while consulting a notebook.

'I see,' he said. 'And your wife made the appointment?'

'Yes.'

'You didn't want to come?' he asked, smiling.

'Shrewd,' I thought to myself. Here was someone who practised the art of deduction as I did myself in my work He could form a hypothesis from a telling detail.

'I'm not a great believer in hypnosis,' I ventured.

He looked at me with interest, but said nothing. The silence was about to become awkward when he spoke again.

'What do you do?'

'I'm a headhunter.'

He nodded, as if my profession was an honourable thing, worthy of note.

'The cigarettes – are they a habit, a response to stress, a pleasure? A little of all three?'

'A little of all three,' I said.

'For how long?'

'Since I was seventeen. The year I sat my *baccalauréat*.'

'Do you remember your first cigarette?'

'Of course.'

'When did you smoke your last one?'

'My last one?' I repeated, in surprise. 'I smoked a cigarette on my way here, out on the street.'

'So there are two points in your story: your first and your last cigarette,' he said. 'Between these two points you have lit thousands of cigarettes. We're going to go back, if you'll allow me, to before the first one, to when you were a non-smoker.'

I stared at him in silence. I found to my surprise that I was closely following his train of thought.

'We're going to go back to before you had the desire,' he said.

'The desire to feel desire,' I joked, parodying Johnny Halliday.

'You could put it like that,' he said, without the flicker of a smile. 'Please make yourself comfortable on the couch.'

He stood up. I did the same, removed my jacket and lay down on the couch.

'You can take your boots off if you wish.'

I slipped them off and lay down again. He sat on the chair beside me. Had someone taken a photograph, it would have looked as if I was recounting my woes to my analyst.

'What are you going to do?'

'Don't be anxious.'

'I'm not.'

'I think you are; I can tell by your voice, but that's quite normal. We're going to go back in time; your mind will link the key moments in your life, the ones connected to smoking cigarettes. By describing them, you will bring them out of your subconscious, and then you can put them away in a small box. And that is how you will rid yourself of the craving to smoke.'

'You mean I'm going to talk to you?' I asked, turning to look at him.

'Yes.'

This hadn't occurred to me. All I knew about hypnosis was gleaned from fairground attractions and TV shows. I had pictured a silent encounter, eyeball to eyeball, after which I would sink into a deep sleep, like Mowgli in the coils of Kaa the swivel-eyed python. I had imagined something quite theatrical, with me in the role of spectator rather than actor. I would talk about myself in my sleep to a total stranger? I immediately thought of the thousand appalling secrets I might divulge, then felt an odd sense of disappointment. I had very little to hide, in truth, beyond a few scraps of confidential information about stock-exchange strategies and future moves in the business world, as yet unknown even to the newshounds at *Les Échos*. What else? The sexual peccadillos of two or three French CEOs who weren't exactly household names. And personally? No mistress, no embezzlement, nothing worth locking away at the back of my mind.

'Does it bother you to talk while you're asleep?' asked Di Caro.

'No. I'm not a closet murderer,' I said at length.

He smiled. I smiled back. The innocence of the angels before the Fall.

He asked me to relax, empty my mind and stare at the sunlight on a wall in the distance, outside the window. I did as he asked and tried to think about nothing, absolutely nothing. The room was silent and pools of sunlight warmed my legs through my trousers.

He told me to concentrate on his voice and picture the images he described.

'You're very far away from here,' he began; 'you're on a beach, far away, very far away, a deserted, sunlit beach; you're all alone and you feel happy. Where are you?'

'In the screen saver on my PC,' I said.

I had downloaded a picture of a beach in the Caribbean, a place to escape between reviewing Word files.

'You're sitting on the sand,' he said. 'You hear the sound of the waves; the water is clear, very clear; the sky is blue, very blue. You look at the sand, the hot sand. Think about the millions of grains of sand; you are the sand, you are a grain of sand on the beach, you are a grain of sand on the beach, you are a grain of sand on the beach, on the beach … beach …'

My mind emptied. I stared at the wall outside in the sunshine. The image of the vast expanse of burning sand filled my mind. I felt good. I was going to fall asleep for sure. Episodes from my life, connected with cigarettes, would float to the surface. I would talk about them out loud, while unconscious. I would see myself at twenty-five, in Monsieur Jacquard's office, see my father and his cigars, my mother's shop, a lighter engraved with a phrase in Spanish, and the first cigarette, the one you never forget. I would see it all over again ... I lost consciousness. The first memory that took the place of the fine sandy beach was that of my first day at HBC, and a name from a long time ago: Jeannine Limarlian. Jeannine Limarlian: 356 76 21.

Since I have no memory of what I told Di Caro, all I can do is piece together the key moments from my past as I think best. The ones that explain why I smoke and who I am. Among the brain's many mysteries, I note that when we try to picture the past, we see ourselves looking as we do today. But I didn't look like I do now, of course, because it was twenty-five years ago.

My 'telephone' period lasted for three years and began one December morning at Beauchamps-Charellier Executive Profiles, the future HBC Consulting. I was being interviewed for the job of assistant to Jean Jacquard, a former screenwriter who, late in his career, had switched to head-hunting and a post as head of research. A curious character with his beige mac, soft felt hat and big horn-rimmed glasses, he was my guide and mentor as I took my first steps in this unknown territory. A landscape of big businesses, with concealed bear traps and land-mines.

'We are the advance party down on the plain, dear boy, do you understand?' he said, in the interview, chewing the stem of his pipe. 'The hunter does not set out until the mines have been cleared and the mist has lifted. It is he who scales the mountain. We stay down on the ground.'

He gesticulated to demonstrate his point, running his hands across his desk. I noticed that there was no superfluous clutter, no accessories – no framed picture of his wife and children, no marble globe or cube acting as a paperweight. Just a telephone, a notepad and a Montblanc pen. It was as if he had never had a life, as if he didn't really exist. He seemed to have stepped straight out of a film in which he played the kind of cameo role with just a handful of lines that leave their mark in the audience's mind nonetheless. He might have been a police informer, or a solicitor, a character whose very presence helps unravel the disentangles the tangled threads of the plot.

'See this telephone – this, and the coffee machine, will be your best friends.'

I stared at the grey telephone, with its rotary dial. The transparent disc full of holes whirred and clicked each time a number was dialled.

'Our job is to identify suitable candidates, then make contact with those selected by the headhunter. Do you understand?'

This was the era of three television channels and no mobile phones, when computer databases were in their infancy and the Internet was a figment of the science-fiction writer's imagination. Potential candidates couldn't be contacted quite as easily as today: they were generally not in the phone book, spent longer working for the same company, frequently fell behind with their subscriptions to their school and college alumni associations, and hence failed to appear in the annual directory of former pupils. Their secretaries, who were only just beginning to be referred to as 'personal assistants', were instructed in the old rules of the game (chiefly, not to disturb their bosses under any circumstances) and they applied them with the zeal of a concierge of a luxury apartment building, the kind that spies on you from behind her net curtains then emerges to bombard you with questions if you spend too long peering at the list of residents' names. 'Are you looking for someone?' We drew on an armoury of telephone tricks, including passing ourselves off as someone else altogether, in order to get through to the target candidate in person. The detective work, gone today but once essential to the job, had a charm all of its own.

Monsieur Jacquard packed his pipe slowly, taking his time, then struck a match. At that exact moment, he made me think of Chief Inspector Maigret. He would have made an ideal choice to play Simenon's character. I often wanted to ask him what films he had worked on, but the subject was taboo for some strange reason. He never spoke about it, and I never found an opportunity to turn the conversation to his screen work. In fifteen years, all I discovered was that he had once worked with Claude Sautet and that he had gone to Hollywood at the request of a famous American director, whose name no one could ever tell me. Jacquard was never mentioned in film histories; he must have used a pseudonym, and as the years went by, I gave up trying to find out what it was.

He stood up and opened a metal storage cabinet. He took out the telephone directory (volume I–Z) and placed it in front of me before returning to his seat. We stared at one another, and the silence lasted for several seconds. I heard the faint sizzle of the tobacco each time he drew on his pipe.

'Choose a page at random,' he said.

I opened the directory. Two pages splayed open in front of me, left and right.

'Pick a man's name at random.'

I decided not to think too hard and bent over the rows of names: Lime, Charles; Limentour, Henri; Limeras, Etienne; Limois, David; Limousin, Jacques …

'Hurry up!' he insisted.

'Jacques Limousin, 83 Boulevard Beaumarchais, in the third arrondissement.'

'Now a woman.'

I pored over the lists. I chose Jeannine Limarlian, 42 bis Rue Belgrand, in the twentieth.

'Good. Now you're going to find out where they both work. The address, the arrondissement, what floor, the office number (if there is one), the entry code to the building (if there is one). You have thirty minutes.'

I must have muttered a few questions, with a vague attempt at humour, because I remember his reply. With his pipe clenched between his teeth, he retorted: 'This isn't a joke.'

Then he left the room and closed the door behind him, adding: 'You may smoke.'

What was I getting into? Thirty minutes for two people, fifteen minutes apiece. Who would tell me where they worked? What they did? Who on earth was Jeannine Limarlian, with a name like that? I had to rise to the challenge. I played the game. I didn't know it would last twenty-five years.

Thirty minutes and seven cigarettes later, Monsieur Jacquard opened the office door and sat down in front of me.

'So?'

'Jeannine Limarlian is a hairdresser, 18 Rue Fabre d'Églantine in the twelfth. The salon's called Jeannine Brushing, telephone number 356 76 21. Jacques Limousin works in customer services at Crédit Lyonnais in Pontoise, 45 Avenue Paul-Vaillant-Couturier. The number is 245 67 97, extension 438.'

He nodded.

'Call Jeannine Brushing.'

'The salon's closed now; she told me she'd be there in an hour.'

'Call her!'

I began dialling. After three digits, a recorded voice told me the number was unobtainable. I stared at Jacquard. I didn't understand. Had the woman lied to me? And if she had, how could

Jacquard know? Because he clearly did know or he wouldn't have asked me to dial the non-existent number. He smiled as if he had just cracked a terrific joke that would have had an imaginary audience in stitches. The office was totally silent.

'Turn the page, young man.'

I turned the page of the telephone directory. It took me a few seconds to realise that the next page was identical. I turned back to the previous page to make sure. There was no doubt about it, both began with 'Lilenstein, Henri' and ended with 'Lina, Albertine'. I checked a few other pages at random. The entire directory consisted of the same two pages. I looked up at Jacquard.

'And that's not all,' he said. 'If you're observant, you will notice that ...'

He left the sentence unfinished — another challenge. What else could I find that was wrong with this fake directory? I pored over the columns of names, losing precious seconds before realising the second problem lay not with the names, but the numbers. The page was filled with just four telephone numbers, two for the men, two for the women. A detail it was impossible to spot at first, because once you choose a name, you only look at the corresponding number. I completed his sentence.

'... there are only four telephone numbers here.'

Jacquard bowed slightly, with a curious expression, part compliment and part 'you took your time'.

'Who are these people?' I asked.

'Who do you think?'

'Your people?'

He smiled at my form of words.

'The numbers belong to the four other research assistants here in the office. All your telephone calls went down to the basement offices right here.'

'You were down there?' The light was dawning, slowly.

'Yes, we put you on the loudspeaker. Clever move, passing yourself off as a tax officer. The radio-quiz trick for the lady has been used before, but it's always effective.'

We looked at each other. One of my father's expressions came into my head: 'A bit of an oddball.' Yes. He was a bit of an oddball all right.

'I'll take you on for a two-month trial period. How does that sound?'

'That sounds great.'

The night before, I had answered an advert in the paper:

HEADHUNTER. *Professional firm seeks capable self-starter for filing and other tasks. Pay commensurate with experience. Bonus a possibility.*

Today, new graduates with their careers all planned out would smile at Jacquard's unorthodox methods. But in my view, his prank – which was already outdated even then – was a formidable test of a candidate's potential. Formidable in its simplicity. Putting someone in an unfamiliar situation tests their ability to get to grips with the unknown and survive. Most species of animal will die if they are taken out of their normal habitat. You have to test their resistance to the shock of the change and be sure to return them to a similar environment. The headhunter does precisely this when he lures his quarry. Will the quarry be captured easily? Will he or she cope with the transition and re-adapt? These are the fundamental questions underpinning my profession. My target candidates must flourish amid the flora and fauna of their new habitat. Ideally, he or she will feel even better there, dig themselves a bigger burrow and extend their hunting ground. But I'm getting ahead of myself. Such ideas only came to me much later when I had scaled the heights of my profession.

I was a capable self-starter, much as I had been an incapable *lycée* student. Unlike others, I cherish no fond memories of inspirational teachers who opened my eyes to the world around me, nurtured my special vocation, and with whom I still exchange the occasional letter, tinged with nostalgia. Far from it. School was profoundly dull. Philosophy was the only subject that sparked even mild interest, though it was disastrously badly taught. I felt a great fondness for Kant, Descartes and the rest, as they tortured themselves with the usual twisted questions, from 'Why are we here?' to 'Are we here, really?' and 'Is what I'm seeing only a figment of my imagination?' Their thinking seemed eminently logical to me and their answers were tinged with humour. I was utterly hopeless at maths and only vaguely interested in history and geopolitics. My philosophical bent saved me and got me my *baccalauréat*. The essay topic was something to do with memory and inevitably, ironically, I have absolutely no recollection of what I wrote. Law or philosophy? I wavered for a few months. I began studying philosophy, then switched to law. But neither discipline opened many doors for me, and at twenty-five, after two years as a solicitor's filing clerk, I found myself in the sunlit office of the man with the pipe and the fake telephone directory.

After my first proper job, I had occasionally tutored *lycée* students in *philo*. Most understood nothing of the simple concepts I tried to explain. Their brains were as receptive to Kant's phenomena and noumena as mine was to infinite equations. We each played our parts: I was the student intellectual, dispensing pearls of wisdom, while the spotty schoolkid on the receiving end of my lectures struggled to understand at least some of what I said, and his parents absolved themselves of all responsibility for his future failure. They would have tried anything, however futile. The aim was not to open the overstuffed student mind (so roundly condemned by Montaigne) to the wider world, but to negotiate a kind of civil truce that suited all three parties. Much later, I applied the fruits of this experience to my work. Peace and success were the ultimate goals in the triangle of the hunter, hunted and client. But at the time, my tutoring served no discernible purpose beyond paying for my cigarettes.

Is the desire to smoke hereditary? The perfect essay topic in philosophy or biology – another discipline that interested me. Of which more later. Answering, I would say that smoking is *perhaps* hereditary, though I would venture no further than that. I've seen too many examples of children who don't smoke when their parents do, and children who smoke but were raised in the clean draughts of a fresh, well-ventilated home, to attempt the unravelling of that particular Gordian knot. My father enjoyed Punch cigars. He was a parsimonious smoker, not in order to protect his health, and still less for fear of polluting the lungs of those around him, but, prosaically, due to their cost. The cigar aficionado pays a heavy price, though his smokes last longer than cigarettes and not all are as costly as a Davidoff or a Montecristo. As a child, I detested the smell of stale tobacco that lingered in our apartment. I found it truly disgusting – a piquant memory for the inveterate smoker I would become. Cigars were ugly and they stank. My father was a true connoisseur: only matches would do to light his cigars. The ritual of warming the tip of the cigar with the lit match until he almost scorched his fingers, then blowing out the match just at the very last moment, made him very happy. But once the broad tip of the cigar glowed, allowing him to exhale clouds of smoke, his anxious frown would return and he would stare vacantly into the distance .

He was tall and thin, with cropped blond hair. The stick in his mouth seemed like a natural extension of his body. His appearance suggested the dynamism of a man in a hurry, full of projects. But this was far from the case. My father was often to be found in the English club armchair he had made his own, in the sitting room, crossing his legs and raising his eyebrows slowly and painfully, as if the action required superhuman effort. He would gather his strength by drawing on his cigar, until his entire being disappeared in the curls of blue smoke.

Viewed from the sofa, the scene had a touch of the surreal, like trick photography in a film. The image that came to mind was of an octopus retreating behind its inky smokescreen, and this was quite apt. My father was an architect and my mother an antiques dealer. They were very much at home in the art world, but they were not interested in the same things. My mother swore by the nineteenth century, while my father was resolutely modern. 'An architect with no buildings to his name,' he would grumble, with a sarcastic smile. His career in no way resembled the imaginings of his younger self. The projects he submitted never came to fruition and, while he always got through the early rounds of the big competitions, he was invariably rejected halfway through the selection process. He made his living redesigning apartment buildings and second homes: an extra room off the kitchen, a veranda, a conservatory. Sometimes he would even see the building of an entire house through to completion, but never according to his original plans. The 'vile bourgeoisie', as he called them (and of which he was a part), never went along with his roof terraces, atria and split-level offices. For years, my father earned less than my mother, and his clients were often people who frequented her antiques shop. The man who wanted to be the next Oscar Niemeyer was unlikely to design the house of the future for these buyers of antique chests of drawers.

I would go walking with him in my early teens. My father would puff on his cigar, while I was allowed a handful of Malabars bought at a bakery along the way. Often, he would remember my bubblegum while he was buying his box of Punch cigars from the tobacco counter in a café. 'Your turn now,' he would say, and we would look around for the nearest bakery. For months, our walks would end at Place du Colonel Fabien. Oscar Niemeyer had drawn up the plans for the headquarters of the French Communist Party, then under construction. I can see my father now, chewing on his cigar, standing motionless, lost in admiration of the great structure. 'It's as if it were floating,' he would murmur, never taking his eyes off it. His long silences invariably ended with the same mysterious phrase: 'And once the dome is in place ...'

Sometimes, our walks took us to Les Halles. Behind the hoardings lay the great expanse of what everyone in Paris called 'the hole'. And a more perfect description of the hectares of waste ground, once the site of Baltard's vast iron and glass pavilions, would have been hard to find. Now it was all mounds and ramps and differing levels, a site bristling with weeds, that was finding it hard to adapt to its new purpose. A small lake had formed in the middle of this mini apocalypse: rubbish and rainwater collected there, and it seemed never to evaporate. Orange mechanical diggers busied themselves here and there like crazed insects. My father would watch the spectacle, his chin firmly set in military fashion, cigar in his mouth, his face once again the silent, tragic mask. He would stay like that for minutes at a time: gradually, the tip of his cigar would turn to a cylinder of ash, to be blown away by the next gust of wind. Then the tip would glow again and the ash would return. Paralysed by his own angst, he stared at heaven knows what imaginary district, building it in his mind, if not in reality. A few years later, another building must have sent his self-esteem plummeting further still: the Centre Pompidou. Renzo Piano joined Niemeyer in his pantheon of figures to be envied. Those pipes, those escalators, like a great, brightly coloured refinery: my father would never have dared. Those architects had struck oil with one stroke of their pen; but the only place my father ever broke ground was his childhood sandpit. He knew this. It was the tragedy of his life.

Years later, searching through a box of books in the cellar, I came across a diary he had kept at the time. Its pages were filled with personal reflections on design concepts of the day, the beginnings of an article on Niemeyer, commissioned by a journal, but which he never finished; figures, too, in columns, and percentages which must have been important on the afternoon he wrote them down, but were meaningless now. A page was devoted to one of his walks to the construction site at Les Halles. He confessed that he had stared into the water-filled hole in the middle until he wished he could end his own life. Until he 'drowned himself there out of sheer rage', to quote his exact words.

I've often wondered if my choice of profession – which consists, ultimately, in helping gifted people find their ideal job – was not inspired, subconsciously, by my father's thwarted career.

When the mysterious dome that had so obsessed him finally sprouted amid the greenery on Place du Colonel Fabien, he was not there to see it. He never did see it. Eighteen months previously, he had left for Cuba to oversee work on a People's Library (a 'media resources centre'). This time, his ideas were dashed not by the vile bourgeoisie, but by their polar opposite: the Cuban Communists. His plans for a library encased in a red Plexiglas bubble had been discarded. The project was of no interest now, he wrote in his letters, 'like everything I've done.' He underlined the phrase twice. The only positive aspect of this distant mission was a constant supply of the finest Havana cigars for the price of his boxes of Punch.

My father met his death on a small road in Cuba. His car was crushed beneath a truck loaded with hundreds of cases of cigars. My mother and I never visited the scene of the accident.

Many times, I looked at the diagram drawn on the police report we received. It showed an empty road, a small rectangle with four circles for my father's car, and a bigger rectangle with four circles for the truck. The small rectangle was moving towards the bigger one on the wrong side of the road, making straight for it, head-on. A Cuban police officer had seen fit to indicate the inevitable direction of the impact with a dotted arrow. The report was admirably thorough: a second arrow indicated the precise point of impact, where he had penned the words '*Aquí la muerte*'. The diagram was signed Manuelito Roblès. I didn't need Manuelito Roblès to tell me that my father had met his death at this precise spot on the diagram. I merely wondered what the Spanish for 'suicide' was, because, in the interest of accuracy, '*aquí el suicidio*' may have been more appropriate. How, on an empty road with no other traffic in sight, can you find yourself on the wrong side, heading straight for a truck which is sounding its horn?

The photos of the accident showed my father's vehicle like a sardine tin that's been crushed underfoot. The truck driver managed to escape before the final explosion, which destroyed cigars worth hundreds of thousands of dollars. My father rose up to heaven in a thick column of smoke, wreathed in the aroma he so loved. When his personal effects were returned, they included a Zippo lighter that had survived the fire. I kept it in my pocket for a long time after. Perhaps 'kept' isn't the right word, because lighters are apt to disappear for long periods. Often, they will hibernate all winter long in the coat cupboard, in a summer-jacket pocket, where a lighter lost in September will be found again the following June. One side of the lighter had Castro's head printed on it in red, while the other bore the legend '*Siempre tiene razón el Líder Máximo!*' engraved in black. The Great Leader and his media resources

My mother and I put my father's smoking paraphernalia away in the top of a cupboard: gold or stainless-steel cigar cutters, ashtrays of various kinds, and a box of cigars that no one would smoke now.

My mother was an elegant, distant woman, her blond hair streaked with grey. I never saw her in anything but trousers. They gave her a masculine air which contrasted with her sweet face. Looking back over the years, putting seemingly insignificant details together, I wondered if my mother hadn't preferred women. She never remarried and, to my knowledge, she never had a liaison with another man. I asked her about it one day. We were talking about one of her friends who had remarried and, naturally, I asked her if she had any desire to do the same. She didn't seem surprised by my question. She frowned and gazed out through the shop window at the other side of the street.

'You know, men ...' she said, wearily. 'I spent twenty years with your father. But, well, you know what your father was like.'

She made a small movement with her hand and didn't finish her sentence. The ensuing silence symbolised the void that had characterised their relationship. We stayed there in the shop, her behind her Empire desk, me sitting on a stool. Outside, cars drove past in the street. *You know what your father was like ...* Yes, I did know. My father, whose architectural projects had never seen the light of day, had been profoundly unhappy, centre had taken my father from me. There was nothing I could do about it. No point in staging a revolt or doing anything at all. The *Líder Máximo* was always right. It said so on the lighter.

My mother and I put my father's smoking paraphernalia away in the top of a cupboard: gold or stainless-steel cigar cutters, ashtrays of various kinds, and a box of cigars that no one would smoke now.

My mother was an elegant, distant woman, her blond hair streaked with grey. I never saw her in anything but trousers. They gave her a masculine air which contrasted with her sweet face. Looking back over the years, putting seemingly insignificant details together, I wondered if my mother hadn't preferred women. She never remarried and, to my knowledge, she never had a liaison with another man. I asked her about it one day. We were talking about one of her friends who had remarried and, naturally, I asked her if she had any desire to do the same. She didn't seem surprised by my question. She frowned and gazed out through the shop window at the other side of the street.

'You know, men …' she said, wearily. 'I spent twenty years with your father. But, well, you know what your father was like.'

She made a small movement with her hand and didn't finish her sentence. The ensuing silence symbolised the void that had characterised their relationship. We stayed there in the shop, her behind her Empire desk, me sitting on a stool. Outside, cars drove past in the street. *You know what your father was like* … Yes, I did know. My father, whose architectural projects had never seen the light of day, had been profoundly unhappy,

centre had taken my father from me. There was nothing I could do about it. No point in staging a revolt or doing anything at all. The *Líder Máximo* was always right. It said so on the lighter.

burdened by his profession. And when people are unhappy, they can never bring joy to anyone else. They become nothing but tenants in their own lives, with no possibility of moving anywhere bigger or more luxurious. They resign themselves to their three-rooms-and-a-kitchen under the eaves, and then escape into the pages of luxury magazines offering sensational apartments with incredible services that they will never be able to buy. They torment themselves by imagining the life they do not have. My father's professional life had become a confining cell, from which he contemplated palaces he would never enter. His only consolation on his long road to Calvary was his faithful cigars.

My mother died in her shop. Her great friend, the woman who ran the bookshop in the next street, found her seated at her Empire desk. Her shop was the only one in the street with its lights still on, that evening. 'She looked as if she was thinking,' the bookseller told me. She had been thinking since the beginning of the afternoon. The doctor's verdict as to the time of death proved that no one had come through the door of the shop since her return from lunch. People had passed by its window; some had perhaps stopped to look, but no one had wanted to disturb the antiques dealer, sitting with her elbows resting on her desk, apparently deep in thought. The closure and sale of the shop to a luxury perfumier fetched more than I could possibly have imagined.

The smell of the place is what I remember most: wax with a hint of turpentine, mingled with her perfume, Poivre by Caron, which was oddly redolent of cloves rather than pepper. The whole bouquet distilled the essence of her clientele: timeless chic, natural elegance and, above all, the insouciance of people who have never wanted for anything, and never will. Money has always smelled of beeswax and cloves to me. When I considered how many thousands of euros my target candidates could demand in salary, I thought in thousands of cloves. The aroma grew stronger and headier with each new zero.

It seems to me that smokers are highly sensuous creatures, in fact, with a 'nose' every bit as developed as that of a professional perfume-maker. Yet paradoxically, suicidally, they delight in wrecking it, packet by packet, year after year. If wax and cloves was the smell of money, soon another smell would become more important still: the smell of tobacco.

Before I come to my first encounter with cigarettes, I should like to elaborate on a point that was not really mentioned at my trial. I had a passion that might have profoundly changed the course of my existence had I made it my profession.

At the end of my memorable interview with Monsieur Jacquard, I asked him what it was in my application that had caught his eye.

'The "Interests and Activities" section on your CV, dear boy,' he said.

Under 'Interests and Activities', I had put: 'Herpetology: observing and keeping reptiles and amphibians'.

'There's a hint of the hunter there,' he had added.

He had read between the lines of my exceedingly ordinary CV. Had he glimpsed the headhunter I would become? I have no idea. Certainly, when I was writing it, I had hesitated before mentioning my interest. An interest in tennis or golf would have been better, it seemed to me. But I had made the right decision, as it turned out. Consequently, the 'interests and activities' section of a candidate's CV was always one of the things I looked at carefully. I remember one unsuccessful applicant who had written 'swinger' there. It had taken me a few seconds to realise that he was referring to the practice of partner-swapping. I was surprised that the candidate, who had an excellent professional record, had chosen to include this on his CV. I would have liked to meet him to understand why he had included something so provocative, but he was rejected immediately. I tracked his subsequent progress online: he seemed to be managing a small porn empire based in California, ranging from a swingers' club in Canada to amateur film production in Los Angeles. As it turned out he had been right to indicate his tastes. Never lie – that's one of the cardinal rules. Only the weak lie. But the system is self-correcting: they are sucked down into the quicksand of unemployment.

I have mentioned that I believe the right professional culture is important if my target candidates are to flourish in their new environments. My ideas come from my observations of the animal world. Flora and fauna are scarce in central Paris, and this was doubtless the origin of my passion. As a little boy growing up in the city, I suppose I dreamt of the great open spaces that I would never cross on my dull journey to school. Here, in town, a Yorkshire terrier carried on its mistress's arm is a far more common sight than a royal python. My first observations were of stuffed animals. I knew Deyrolle, the famous shop on the Rue du Bac, not far from my mother's. But the motionless polar bears and tigers were of no interest to me. They were too big, too abstract, in a way. Small moving things fascinated me far more. Among the objects my mother bought for her shop was a curious glass box. It contained about ten frogs, stuffed and positioned in human attitudes, recreating an extraordinarily lifelike bistro scene. It had everything: frogs seated at the bar, others playing cards, still others busy at work in the kitchens. The 'curio' was worth a small fortune, and held me rapt for an entire afternoon. One of the figures, a frog smoking a cigarette, had come away from the ensemble and I was allowed to handle it, with the greatest care.

'Do frogs smoke?' I asked.

'No, frogs don't smoke, Fabrice. Can't you see, it's a sort of fairy story?' said my mother.

If they didn't smoke, then what did they do in real life? The stuffed creature, in its human pose, a cigarette between its slender round-ended fingers made a great impression on me. That evening, I started reading a big book on animals that had been left lying around in my father's study. There were several photographs of frogs and precise descriptions of their anatomy and habits.

The next weekend was spent at my grandparents' country house in Sologne. We didn't keep the property for long, and my memories of it are vague. But I clearly remember a pond at the edge of the nearest village. We had stopped there once when our car had broken down. After a good half an hour waiting expectantly for my father's return, my mother had given vent to her feelings.

'He's gone off to buy cigars again!' she declared, slamming the car door.

Taking advantage of the long wait, with no sign of anyone coming to our aid, I had approached the edge of the pond to observe the area around it. A frog was croaking, heedless of my presence. A green tree frog, identical to the one that had been stuffed and posed by the author of the bistro scene in my mother's glass case. This one was far more interesting than her town cousin, the desiccated smoker. If only I could somehow magically remove a piece of the pond and take it to my bedroom. For the future herpetologist, the idea of taking a sample of nature, like a living three-dimensional Polaroid, is the first sign of his nascent passion.

The plastic cup I had been clutching in my hand since the beginning of the journey still held a little water, and proved an excellent receptacle for the tree frog. Twenty minutes later, we were driving to the house; I kept the palm of my hand firmly over the top of the cup, from which there now came a croaking sound not usually heard in our car.

'Throw that vile thing away!' ordered my mother.

'It's your fault,' said my father, chewing a cigar that he had indeed bought more than a kilometre from the scene of our breakdown. 'You shouldn't have shown him that amphibians' graveyard of yours.'

'It's not a graveyard, Jacques, it's a curio. It'll pay for this holiday, may I remind you,' she retorted.

My mother said this without meaning to hurt, but my father's jaw remained clenched until he went to bed.

That evening, I put the tree frog in an old aquarium hastily filled with earth and Evian water, separating the liquid and the solid with a piece of cardboard. I had created a terrarium, though I didn't know it at the time.

Five or six months later, my bedroom was full of terrariums piled one on top of the other, almost up to the ceiling, carefully organised according to the species they contained: frogs, snakes, lizards, chameleons. Other children played with their dogs or cats, but I liked my exotic creatures. I never once considered my specimens as pets. Even today, I loathe the sight of some eccentric walking down the street with a ferret on their shoulder, calling it Hector and being quite the attraction at the café on the corner. Likewise Goth girls who accessorise their outfit with a python called Nathalie, and take them with them when they go to hip nightclubs. These simpletons call their creatures emotional-support animals. As far as I'm concerned, they are fools who understand nothing.

There was one unbreakable rule at home: no poisonous animals allowed. Nothing dangerous, nothing with so much as a drop of venom. I only broke it once. The golden poison frog – scientific name *Phyllobates terribilis* – was just too lovely. My unsuspecting parents had no idea. I swore the little creature – barely longer than half my thumb – was harmless. The lemon-yellow *Phyllobates terribilis* took up residence in the terrarium formerly occupied by my unfortunate python.

Originally from South America, *Phyllobates terribilis* is one of the most dangerous animals in the world, used by certain indigenous tribes as a source of poison for their arrows. It has no venom, but is technically poisonous, because its three square centimetres of skin hold enough toxins to kill ten men in their prime. Place one finger on it and you will die within thirty minutes of muscular paralysis, with all the symptoms of an embolism, coupled with a heart attack. Make contact for just a few seconds and the countdown begins.

I kept it for a year and a half. When I disposed of its body, with a thousand precautions, I never imagined that this unique boyhood transgression would serve me thirty-five years later. For a far greater transgression altogether.

And so not only had my interests as noted on my CV opened the door to my future career, they had also, without me knowing it, been an apprenticeship of sorts. Reptiles, amphibians and my careful observation of them had been my gateway to the observation of top-finance directors and other high-flying executives. My office at HBC was little more than a giant virtual terrarium. The rare, exotic species I hunted were no longer coiled lazily behind the glass of their tanks, but scrupulously filed behind my computer screen, each in his box, or folder. I knew their favourite diet, their preferred habitat. My knowledge of the animal kingdom had been the ideal training ground for life as a manhunter.

From smoking frog to boa constrictor, my hike through this

marvellous terrain lasted more than twenty years. My marriage put an end to a passion that had already waned, truth be told, for lack of time.

But let us return to my last days as a non-smoker, because it was this door in particular that Marco Di Caro intended to open during my artificially induced sleep.

I was seventeen years old, an amateur philosopher, confirmed herpetologist and future law student. I was desperately bored. There was nothing unusual about any of that.

I achieved a mediocre *baccalauréat*, having failed to shine in the oral exams. My efforts in the whole perilous undertaking, which mainly seemed to involve stress and insomnia, were not rewarded with a good mark. On results day, I headed for the hall of a local *lycée* (not my own) and searched for my name on the list of successful candidates. I can still feel the anguish that gripped me that day. The frisson and breathlessness I experienced as I read down the list. Vabier, Vacquinot, Vaffier, Vagon, Vaillerdier, until at last I saw Valantine. Valantine, Fabrice. There I was. I was saved. With hindsight, I wonder how I could possibly have faced the experience without lighting up a cigarette that very minute. At the time, I didn't smoke. After so many years wreathed in clouds of blue smoke, my early days as a non-smoker are a mystery. How could I tackle the anxieties and unforeseen eventualities of everyday life without putting my hand into my jacket pocket and taking out my packet of cigarettes? I really can't understand how I did it. For seventeen years, I didn't smoke: hence I was able to spend hours poring over texts by Descartes or the history of the Second World War without a nicotine fix to boost my brain. It was a feat, an achievement. I was able to concentrate on the pages and the topic without reaching for my lighter. A few years later, this would have been unthinkable. So I associate a cigarette-free life with childhood and adolescence.

With my *baccalauréat* newly acquired and my lungs as yet fresh and clean, I spent the month of August in Normandy. My mother sent me to stay with some family friends, while she went to Istanbul with her bookseller friend. I found myself staying with the Larnaudy family, in a vast farmhouse in the Auge. It had been a long time since anyone had milked a cow here. The house and its outbuildings had been transformed into a second home, where the owners came to rest and breathe the country air, far from the pressures and responsibilities of life in Paris. The old stables now housed a ping-pong table and a minibar, the huge barn was a building site, with plans for a swimming pool, and the main farmhouse had a state-of-the-art kitchen, and many bedrooms and bathrooms. Agricultural chores had long since been superseded by the languorous activities of the middle classes on holiday. Early-morning animal feeding had given way to the leisurely breakfasts of a family, none of whom had experience of rabbit hutches or hungry foxes on the prowl. For me, the holiday was a curious interlude, when time stood still, as if suspended in the haze of summer. Looking back, I can identify the powerful feelings of anxiety I felt that August: my whole life lay before me. A strange sensation that can only be felt for a short period in our existence. After that, it's too late: life catches up. The future becomes blurred, we exist only in the present, yet we find ourselves running constantly in order to stand still. That summer, the present was non-existent, and the future was far in the distance. I would give all the gold I don't possess to go back to that moment in time.

Larnaudy père was an old school friend of my father's. When he had drunk too much whisky, he would tell me things about my father. His memories would rise bit by bit, like divers returning to the surface in stages from the deep.

'Your father is a great fellow,' he would say, swinging his glass.

He launched with relish into the story of one of my father's projects, from a few years before. He had, it seemed, drawn up the plans for a series of infinity pools that would descend in steps down the sloping farmhouse grounds.

'A fabulous project! Revolutionary!' enthused Larnaudy *père*. 'But too complicated to build, far too expensive as well,' he said reproachfully, in his next breath.

He was singing the praises of a scheme he had refused to finance. It was through meeting adults like him that I began to seriously doubt human nature and, I admit, to show it rather less respect. I was well past my seventeenth birthday, and leaving my childhood behind forever, but what I saw of the adult world was making me cynical: men who spent their time pontificating, and mulling over their failures and memories. They seemed like incompetent idiots, to me.

Four of us had passed our *bac* that summer: Charlotte Larnaudy, her friend Marie, her brother Olivier and me.

One evening, we found ourselves alone in the big farmhouse. The parents had gone for dinner with friends and we had reheated the leftovers from lunch. We had abandoned plans to go to a nightclub in Deauville – it was late and we were all tired from helping to cut down a tree that afternoon. We couldn't watch TV as the aerial had been damaged during a storm and the parents hadn't had it repaired.

It was Olivier, I believe, who suggested we all play Monopoly. We began with little enthusiasm, but gradually the game took hold. I have no idea who won and who lost: my memory of the little red hotels and prestigious streets is blurred by the bottle of 75-per-cent-proof Calvados we had taken from the dresser. Illegal liquor, distilled in secret, and sold to order in the countryside. We drank small shots, one after the other. Even now, I can taste the flavour of cooked apple and fiery woodsmoke that dried our mouths and made us want another glass immediately. Marie took out a packet of cigarettes and lit one. A packet of Dunhill Red. She offered me one. I refused. A moment later, the other three were all smoking.

'Haven't you ever had a cigarette?' asked Charlotte.

'Oh yes … I have. Sometimes. My dad smokes cigars, but I don't like it.'

'Cigars are disgusting. Cigarettes are different,' said Marie.

'I really like cigars,' said Olivier.

I had lied. Why had I pretended to have tried cigarettes? No doubt to avoid teasing or snide remarks. Non-smokers were not exactly cool, back then, and adolescents were notoriously boastful, and taunting. In any case, I was about to put an end to my lie. What led me to reach out, take a cigarette and light it? The urge to try one, that's all. Spurred on by the euphoria induced by too much Calvados, no doubt. And the impression that my whole life lay before me. The desire to be like everyone else? I don't think so. It was more that I didn't want to stand out from the others, all of whom smoked. Why not give it a try? My mother wasn't there, nor the senior Larnaudys; I wasn't in my own home: sometimes when we are out of our normal surroundings, we act differently. We do things we wouldn't do elsewhere.

I'd often heard it said that the first puffs of tobacco make a new smoker cough. I didn't want to draw attention to myself around the table and I wanted to be able to stifle any coughing without it being too obvious.

'I'm taking a break, play for me,' I told them.

I took the Bic lighter and the cigarette protruding from the packet and went to sit some distance away, in front of the fire. The flames had died down in the hearth, leaving only a few embers glowing between the firedogs. The old leather club armchair was comfortable, and the fireplace radiated a pleasant heat, matching the glow from the Calvados in my belly. My glass had been gently warming. I drank it down in one and placed it on a rustic three-legged stool close by. I sniffed the long white stick with its smell of dry tea, raised it to my lips and clicked the lighter. I remember it was a few seconds before I realised I was supposed to breathe in for the tip to light up. That was it, now the cigarette was burning. I stared at it in my hand, like some incongruous extension of my body. The smoke spiralled up into the air. I drew on the cigarette, then breathed the smoke straight out again, without inhaling. As extraordinary as this may seem, I didn't know you were supposed to inhale; I thought everyone did what I was doing now. It wasn't unpleasant, quite the opposite. It was new, and much more fun than drinking a glass of champagne. I had spent time with plenty of smokers, but had never wanted to smoke. Now I was doing just that. It was like walking past a magnificent sports car parked on the street every day for years, and then suddenly, magically, finding you have the keys in your pocket.

I gazed into the embers in the fireplace. I felt great. Could I exhale the smoke through my nose, like the other hardened smokers did? The first attempt scorched my nostrils slightly, but I managed it. But the smoke seemed determined to attack my eyes: the tiniest wisp would go straight into to them, leaving a nasty stinging sensation, like a trickle of shampoo under your eyelid. When that happens, you need to splash your eyes with quantities of clean water. With smoke, all you can do is blow discreetly upwards, over your face. You do that at first, but after a while, the smoke doesn't hurt your eyes any more. It behaves. It understands that it mustn't go anywhere near them.

I shifted sideways in the armchair to avoid the problem of getting smoke in my eyes. A long, thin curl rose to the ceiling. I could hear the others talking and laughing, the sound of the small plastic dice on the board. Their voices came to me from far away. I blew the smoke far out in front of me, into the embers. The first hit of nicotine filtered into my veins and reached my brain. Smoking heightened my sense of well-being. It's certainly true that in your first years as a smoker, cigarettes have a wonderful ability to intensify the moments associated with them. After that, the feeling diminishes. My head spun slightly, but this wasn't a migraine, just a slight woozy feeling. I thought of nothing. I was far from everything. I felt great. My chemical love affair with cigarettes had begun.

'Fabrice? Hey, Fabrice! Bad news ...'

'What?' I murmured, keeping my eyes closed.

'You're in jail!'

The phrase was not without a certain piquancy, in light of subsequent events. Yes, what started that summer would land me in jail one day. As if that first cigarette was already associated with crime and punishment. That very evening, when we all went to bed, Marie noticed her packet was empty. I had smoked them all. When you have a talent for something, you just know straight away.

We went into town the next day, and for the first time in my life I entered a café to buy cigarettes. At the counter, I stared at the dozens of packets lined up on the shelves: the cigars and cigarillos at the top, loose tobacco for pipes and roll-ups at the bottom, and in between, occupying by far the largest space, Virginia cigarettes, then a smaller display of dark-tobacco cigarettes. I was impressed by the number of different packet designs and colours. 'So many different ways of presenting exactly the same thing,' I thought. My smoking career would teach me that no two cigarette brands are the same. To say that all cigarette packets contain the same thing would be tantamount to saying that all blonde women look alike. Like her counterparts in flesh and blood, the good fairy Nicotine has a thousand faces: a Marlboro Red has nothing in common with a Benson & Hedges Gold, which is nothing like a Philip Morris Blue, itself utterly unlike a Dunhill.

The years that followed often saw me queuing up in the most important part of any café – the tobacco counter. Just as airport departure lounges look the same the world over – the preserve of globetrotting travellers, to the extent that some even escape the reach of international law – so, too, those three square metres are the same wherever you go. The empty packet you crumpled and threw away when you left Paris or Rome will be waiting, shiny and full, in Tokyo or New York. It's one of the great certainties of life, like nightfall, the passage of time, and the promise of sunshine in summer.

A good tobacco counter is a tobacco counter with no one else waiting. Queueing is unbearable. The few minutes wasted are worse even than those spent waiting for the next metro when the previous train has just left the platform. Buying a packet of cigarettes has all the ritual solemnity of a game of poker: you stake your money, retrieve the packet, claim your change. Three distinct actions performed with the precision of a casino croupier over the high glass-topped counter. Polite, dextrous, these gestures take only a few seconds.

Smokers' solidarity reigns while waiting at the tobacco counter. But intruders are a constant nuisance, including two particularly noxious species. There's the phone-card buyer, who invariably requires detailed and lengthy explanations about costs and whether the card will work abroad. Unbearable. But the Palme d'Or goes to the gamblers: with their boxes to tick and their cards to scratch, these dreamers honestly believe they can be billionaires by scraping furiously with their thumbnail, losing the smokers – who have no time to spare – valuable minutes. How many times have I tutted in exasperation and sighed to indicate that I'm waiting, behind one of their number as they hesitate between an Astro, a Millionnaire or a Keno card? The very worst specimen of this lowest of breeds is the one who comes to claim his winnings on a dozen different cards, barely covering his initial outlay. While the tobacconist carefully totals each amount, over a period of several minutes, the line of smokers grows longer. I tut, and sigh, and others sigh with me, but all to no avail. Faces darken, watches are checked. Images flash in our minds in which we jostle the man who is taking his time and making us waste ours, we shove him out of the queue, we remonstrate with him, pelt him with our empty packets and lighters, set fire to him there and then. Does the smoker's rush of annoyance carry with it the seeds of murder? My lawyer cautiously sidestepped the issue. But it merits closer examination, in my view.

'A packet of Dunhill Red, king-size,' I said to the big blonde woman behind the counter.

I chose a simple plastic lighter with a picture of a Normandy cow. The sum requested would raise a smile today when prices have risen to such stratospheric heights.

I made my purchase as if it were second nature to me. The small voice that told me 'Don't do it' had been silenced the minute I stepped through the café door. I lit my first cigarette out on the street that day and found that the slim white stick in my hand gave me a certain presence. Psychoanalysts have constructed numerous theories around the cigarette as a substitute for the child's thumb, cuddly toy, security blanket, even its mother's breast, elaborating on every possible emotional deficiency lurking behind the blue smokescreen. I tend to agree. Cigarettes enter our lives as companions, loyal friends waiting for us at every street corner, ready to walk a few steps of the way with us in exchange for a handful of coins. And when they are gone, an identical packet replaces the last one and quickly finds a place in our pockets alongside other essentials such as our wallet or our house keys. Smokers can seriously harm others around them, but they offer a number of advantages for their friends and partners, too. On birthdays and in the festive season, their workmates and their nearest and dearest are never lacking for gift ideas: a fine vintage ashtray, an elegant lighter, a box of cigars. And the smoker suits every pocket: from a souvenir ashtray to a gold Cartier lighter, the range of accessories is inexhaustible. Over the years, I've amassed an impressive and entirely unintentional collection of all the top brands: Dunhill, Cartier, Dupont, in gold or stain-less steel, silver or bright-red enamel. But I'm forever running short of gas, or flints, or fuel, so that now I prefer the legendary colourful plastic Bic to my battery of luxury lighters.

That evening steeped in bootleg Calvados had introduced me to cigarettes, but I still hadn't understood how to inhale the smoke. Less than a week later, the revelation came, and I have to tell you how it happened.

There was more than a touch of the Biblical about it. The sense of sin and transgression was palpable. It was all there, even the snake which turned up uninvited.

The holiday was coming to an end and I was walking alone, on a sultry afternoon, in the forest beside the Larnaudys' property. The parents and their son had gone into town, and Charlotte and her friend Marie were visiting an old abbey out in the country. I remember clearly the quasi-mystical sense of solitude I felt as I wandered through the cool rooms of the house. I had smoked a cigarette on the steps leading to the garden, gazing up at the sky. I had nothing to do. Nothing planned for the day, nor for the days ahead. At the end of the week, I would be returning to Paris and tackling the as yet unresolved question of my enrolment at university. But for now, all that seemed far away, very far away, in the infinite distance of the future. The trees rustled in a gentle, warm breeze and I closed my eyes in the sunshine, just as I would years later, in the prison yard. Though my eyes were closed, I saw a reddish glow and sensed the light and heat of summer.

I decided to take a walk, not too far, obviously, because I wasn't familiar with the footpaths and nearby woods. I locked the house with the key that had been given to me in case I wanted to go out, and left a note on the table saying where I was going and the time I had left.

As I entered the forest, I wondered if I would come across

any animals of interest. With a population chiefly of rodents and birds, I was unlikely to find many of my favourite specimens. Perhaps a few lizards, maybe even a snake. I walked along footpaths shrouded in absolute silence; even the leaves underfoot made no sound as I passed. I reached a clearing and decided to sit on a tree stump and smoke a cigarette. The idea of a cigarette as a reward is very important to a smoker. We talk of treating ourselves to a cigarette. The curious notion of pleasure in the act of self-medication is one of the keys to tobacco consumption: we are the donkey plodding towards the carrot held in front of its nose, except that in our case there is no master dangling our reward on the end of a stick. Our personal carrot is in our jacket pocket and its lighter is never far away.

I lit my cigarette with my Bic. Already I was looking for a suitable spot to stub it out on the stump. I didn't want to start one of those summer fires that ravage the forests. A crevice in the wood would be fine, then all I would need to do was remove the stub and slip it into my pocket. The smoke rose through a shaft of sunlight and I felt good, still in that tranquil state of inner emptiness that comes from hours on end without speaking to anyone. Hearing and saying nothing can be beneficial for some, but causes anxiety in others. I would rediscover these hours of stillness in my prison cell.

The silence was suddenly interrupted. I heard a girl's voice call out in the forest, followed by stifled laughter, then nothing. I was not alone, although I couldn't see anyone. I rose from my seat on the tree stump. Strange. I hadn't dreamt it, I had heard the girl's voice, and she was obviously close by but I still couldn't see her. I moved silently towards a coppice of small trees, parched by the August sun. The smoke from my cigarette rose in the sunlight. I approached the coppice. It concealed a small mossy hollow and in it, lying stretched out, stark naked on a tartan blanket, were Charlotte Larnaudy and her friend Marie. Their clothes were strewn here and there among the branches. Charlotte Larnaudy bent over her friend, murmuring something in her ear before delicately circling it with the tip of her tongue. Her friend placed a hand on her thigh, caressing her, and the two rolled around on top of each other. I watched the scene, transfixed. I feel sure my eyes stared wider than normal, the better to imprint the vision on my retina and store it in my brain, never to be forgotten. Charlotte had buried her head between her friend's thighs. Her bobbed blond hair swung gently back and forward with the rhythmic movements of her neck. The other girl threw her head back, removed her sunglasses and closed her eyes. Her lips were parted and she gave regular sighs. Very carefully, I crouched down among the leaves, raised my cigarette to my lips and took a drag. Marie gasped and I found myself doing the same: the smoke was sucked into my lungs. My head spun as never before. I breathed out and the smoke was expelled, hanging in the air as if suddenly it was fifteen degrees below zero and my breath was freezing on the air. So this was what they meant by inhaling? The smoke going in and out of the lungs in a perfectly controlled movement that did not make you cough. By chance, I had discovered the smoker's ultimate goal, and the tremendous kick it produced. I did it again, at once. Again, my head spun, but my eyes remained fixed on the two girls.

Minutes passed and the girls were still kissing and caressing each other when I detected a movement in the leaves, a few metres from their blanket. I saw a perfectly controlled curve that I knew at once having observed it so many times. It was a snake. I stared from the girls to the snake and back. It had emerged from the leaves and I recognised its markings: *Natrix natrix*, a big grass snake with a white collar, utterly harmless. It moved towards the tartan blanket and was soon on top of it, a few centimetres from Marie's bare foot. The foot moved and, in so doing, made contact with the reptile's small pointy head. Swift as lightning, *Natrix natrix* sank its teeth into the heel. I can still hear Marie's piercing scream today, and Charlotte's immediately afterwards. There was pure panic. The snake disappeared as only they know how, slithering quickly back into the undergrowth. Marie began to cry loudly and Charlotte followed suit, as she examined the bite.

'It can't be, it can't be, it can't be,' stuttered Charlotte, like a stuck record.

The two stared at one another in terrified silence. I sensed their dismay, the product of irrational yet perfectly understandable fear. The words just slipped out: 'It's not dangerous.'

Charlotte Larnaudy turned in my direction. I stepped out of my hiding place.

'It's not dangerous,' I said again. 'Nothing to worry about. It was a ring-necked grass snake, they aren't poisonous.'

They stared, caught between relief and disbelief at the sight of me there. Charlotte Larnaudy gulped.

'Were you watching us?' she asked, weakly.

I raised my eyebrows.

'Not on purpose,' I said, in my defence. 'I came out for a walk.'

Charlotte stretched out her hand, picked up her T-shirt and covered her breasts.

'Thanks,' said Marie.

Charlotte turned to stare at her.

'Yes, thank you,' Marie insisted. 'Fabrice knows everything about those vile creatures, and I'd rather know I'm OK than think I'm about to die.'

'Yeah, of course,' whispered Charlotte.

At that moment I felt a sharp bite between my fingers. My cigarette had burned down to the filter and scorched me. I dropped it, swore loudly and crushed it under my heel.

'Show the forest some respect,' said Charlotte, who had recovered her spirits somewhat.

'Absolutely. That wasn't deliberate either,' I said, picking up the butt.

'Fabrice.' Charlotte was staring me straight in the eye. 'You won't say anything?'

'He can keep a secret,' said Marie, massaging her foot.

I nodded in silence.

'How long have you been sitting there for?' asked Charlotte.

'I don't know.'

And it was true, I had lost all notion of time. The situation was becoming stranger and stranger. I was talking to two naked girls in the middle of a forest, having just discovered they were in love, and with that, their most precious, intimate secret.

'Come and sit with us, our saviour and voyeur!' said Marie.

She patted the blanket as she spoke, making room for me between the two of them.

I stood motionless.

'Are you scared, or something?'

Stung by the remark, I descended the mossy slope and sat down between them. I had never been this close to a naked girl before, and now here were two of them. Charlotte's breasts were small and firm, Marie's were heavier and pear-shaped. And since we're in the realm of new discoveries and shameful revelations, I should stress that, obviously, at this point, I had never slept with a girl. Another matter that I had assumed would be attended to in the misty future that awaited me at the end of this summer.

Charlotte lit a cigarette and I noted that, unlike me just a few minutes before, she clearly knew very well how to inhale and exhale smoke. A detail that had escaped me before. She held her cigarette out to me and I took a drag, saying nothing. Again, in the fraction of a second, my heart beat faster and my head spun. I passed the cigarette to Marie.

After her first puff, gazing into the forest, she said: 'You know, we like boys too.'

I stared at her, but her eyes met Charlotte's. Charlotte smiled and made as if to gaze into the forest like her friend.

'Lucky that snake came along, wasn't it?' And she burst out laughing.

We all laughed out loud, and when the laughter subsided, I felt Charlotte's mouth placing a kiss on my neck. A moment later, four hands began delicately pulling open the buttons of my shirt.

My summer of vice was complete. The cigar-hating non-smoker I once was had been replaced by a quasi-professional smoker of cigarettes. Behind the serene façade of this respectable middle-class family, girls slept with each other and invited their male friends to join in. I never told a soul what had happened, and when my successive girlfriends, and ultimately my wife, asked me about my first time, after recounting theirs, I would tell them everything – the forest, the cigarette, the snake. Except I would forget to mention that there had been two girls. In my account, there was only ever one.

I saw them again just a couple of times during my first year at university. We never re-enacted the interlude in the forest. Marie left Charlotte Larnaudy after that, and I lost touch with them both. Years later, I saw that Marie was presenting a game show on TV. She became famous and hosted several programmes over a decade or so. During one, a snake charmer was invited into the studio. Just as she was about to stroke the creature live on camera, I felt sure she and I were both thinking about the same episode in our lives.

'Fabrice can keep a secret,' she had said. I could indeed. I would keep my own in time. Four murders. Who can beat that?

How long had it been since the hypnotist's voice had counted off the grains of sand like beads on a rosary? I had no idea. I opened my eyes to see the window and the expanse of wall, no longer in the sun. My mind was blank, like a traveller after hours fast asleep on a long-haul flight. I felt strangely rested. After a few seconds, I turned to look at Di Caro. Sitting motionless in his chair, he seemed to be fast asleep too. His head was lowered and his eyes were closed.

'Let's sit here for a moment in silence,' he murmured.

I did as he said and rested my head against the couch. No thoughts came to mind, and certainly no thought of smoking a cigarette. 'That's impossible,' I thought. 'It can't be that simple.' I paid two hundred euros in cash and left. I had the afternoon to myself. I wandered as far as Place des Abbesses, in Montmartre. Turning onto a small street, I passed the window of a bric-a-brac shop with a display of collectible ashtrays, bearing the logos of defunct brands: Senior Service, Française, Boyard, Strange Lord, Cléopâtre ... I took it as a bizarre quirk of fate: ashtrays in which thousands of cigarettes had been stubbed out, bearing brand names that were now nowhere to be found. They were mere collectors' items, witnesses to a bygone age. Had cigarettes been consigned to my past? I wasn't sure, but pondering the question led me to a brasserie terrace where I found a spot in the sun and ordered a double espresso. The caffeine woke me from my sleepy, befuddled state. Perhaps I was dreaming. I hadn't been to see the hypnotist, but was fast asleep in bed, with my wife beside me. The hands of my alarm clock hadn't yet reached 8 a.m. Not long now – it would ring soon and I would wake up.

The hot, sweet coffee did not make me want a cigarette. That immediate, quasi-Pavlovian reflex to smoke a cigarette with my coffee was absent. Astounded, I ordered another espresso. Still no urge for a cigarette. I took my pack of Benson & Hedges out of my pocket and put it on the table in front of me with my blue Bic lighter. Would these become strangers to me? Wallet, key ring, diary, cigarettes, lighter and, latterly, my phone were the things I always had with me, making my jacket pockets bulge. I put the cigarettes and lighter back in my pocket. I may not have felt the need to smoke, but I did not want to part with my cigarettes. I would carry them around like talismans. 'When did you smoke your last cigarette?' Di Caro had asked. At once, I saw myself taking a drag outside his building, staring at my reflection in the brass plate. Was that it then? My last cigarette? And my first, the Monopoly game, and the smoke I had inhaled, watching the girls in the forest – had I told him about all that, too? Strangely, it didn't matter. I had become indifferent to everything that ought to have bothered me.

A large man sat down at the next table. The breeze wafted his cigar smoke over to me. A Punch. My father's cigars. Images of him flashed through my mind. I must have told the hypnotist about all that, too.

The man was deep in a telephone conversation: something about fruit and vegetables that should have arrived by ship, in a container, but which had disappeared without trace. The man was angry. He must have been in import–export or perhaps in distribution, probably at the wholesale market in Rungis. He abruptly ended the conversation, probably cutting the man on the other end off mid-explanation. He swore under his breath then took a long drag on his cigar, which sent a cloud of smoke my way.

'Excuse me,' I said. 'Is that a Punch you're smoking?'

He turned to me with a frown.

'No, it's not! It's a Romeo y Julieta. Not the same thing at all. I can tell you're not a smoker.' He summoned the waiter.

Not a smoker? I would have loved to take out my packet of cigarettes and light up right in front of him to show him I knew a thing or two about tobacco. But I had no desire to smoke. The situation seemed so absurd that I wanted it to last a while longer, to make the most of it, like a dream whose thread we pick up again after waking briefly in the middle of the night. We know it's a dream, in which we can make anything happen, anything we like. It doesn't matter, because we know it isn't real.

'It's true, I don't smoke,' I told him seriously. 'I've never smoked a cigarette in my life.'

'And proud of it too, I suppose?' he said, with a scornful smile. 'You're all so pleased with yourselves, you lot with your killjoy laws! Soon I won't even be able to smoke a cigar out here on the terrace. Jack Daniel's,' he said, addressing the waiter.

'It's a healthier world without cigarettes,' I persisted.

He nodded, but pulled a face.

'Of course it is! The world's a much, much better place without cigarettes, without cigars, without alcohol – without *coq au vin* and *pieds de cochon*, too, why not? The world would be a better place if we consumed everything *light*, don't you think? That's what your lot like: sugar-free, smoke-free, bourbon-free. You keep to your vegetable garden, Monsieur, and I'll thank you to leave me to my prehistoric cave! I like my wine red, my smoke blue, and my roast lamb bloody!'

'Monsieur, I think ...'

'I don't give a damn what you think, now let me enjoy my bourbon.'

He shifted in his seat, ostentatiously turning his back on me, and began sipping from the glass the waiter had just placed in front of him. This man had used all the arguments I would normally have cited myself. He felt the same rage towards me as I used to feel towards the non-smokers of this world who, after putting up with a very great deal, had succeeded in imposing their diktat. I needed to make amends. I took out my packet and lighter.

'I am a smoker, in fact,' I told him. I showed him my packet and lighter. 'I've just come from a hypnosis session, to try and give up.'

'What a waste of time!'

'Don't you believe in hypnosis? I was fast asleep, I can assure you.'

'Hypnosis works all right: one of my employees does it. It's a trick of the voice. There's a certain frequency that sends people to sleep. Anyone can do it – you just have to know the trick. Like magic.'

'Perhaps. But the fact is I have no desire to smoke.'

'That's not hypnosis; it's auto-suggestion. It's all in your head.' He pointed a finger at his forehead. 'Your head is sending you signals. Nothing to do with people putting you to sleep. The only person responsible for what's happened is you.'

His phone rang again and he resumed his previous conversation where he had left off. The ship, and his vegetables, had been located, it seemed. I put the money for my two coffees on the table and left the terrace with a small wave of farewell. He did not respond.

I was the one responsible for what had just happened to me? Something most certainly had happened: I hadn't smoked for several hours and had not missed it at all.

When I entered our apartment, I noticed a different smell straight away. Sidonie had opened and aired every room that afternoon, and the scent of fresh flowers floated in the air. She had brought home a bouquet of lilies sent to her by Damon Bricker, in thanks for a eulogising article she had written in *Moderna*. The smell of tobacco that lingered permanently around the place had disappeared, as if it had never been. I noticed that the ashtrays had vanished, too. On the coffee table, a jasmine-scented Diptyque candle glowed in place of the crystal ashtray. The other two ashtrays on the mantelpiece had also disappeared.

'Well?' she said, with a seductive smile.

'I haven't smoked since the session,' I replied.

'How do you feel?'

'Strangely rested, as if I was wrapped in cotton wool.'

Over aperitifs that evening, I felt no need to light a cigarette with my Martini Rosso.

'I'm proud of you,' declared Sidonie.

'You don't have to be proud of me, it's not my doing.'

'Di Caro's a very clever man. Michel Vaucourt hasn't touched a cigarette since he saw him.'

The idea of never smoking another cigarette saddened me, I

admit, and I replied somewhat nostalgically, 'All the same, I feel as if I've lost a part of myself.'

'The most dangerous part, Fabrice,' said Sidonie, gravely.

How could she understand that my cigarettes had been my companions, my loyal friends, always to hand when I was in need of comfort. I had divorced a cherished partner, and not by mutual consent. I should have liked a show of compassion, a minute's silence. I might almost have had one if Emma hadn't come home from school at that moment. No sooner had she appeared in the sitting room than she sank onto the sofa and took a packet of Philip Morris Blue from her jeans pocket.

'It's no smoking here, now,' Sidonie told her.

'What the hell?' Emma fired back. 'What's that all about?'

'First of all, don't speak to us like that, and, secondly, your father has stopped smoking.'

'He's stopped twenty times before,' said Emma. 'He never manages more than three days.'

'Your father has been to see a hypnotist, and it's worked! And we'll send you for hypnosis, too, if you don't stop smoking now.'

Emma stared at her mother, intrigued.

'And while you're under, we'll cut off those hideous plaits,' Sidonie continued.

'They're called dreadlocks. Why are you being so aggressive?'

'Your mother's right, you promised to stop smoking when we had dinner at the Jules Verne,' I reminded her.

'While I'm on holiday!' Emma snapped. 'I'll stop when I go to Barcelona, that was our deal. Until then, I'm allowed to smoke!'

'Well, the rules have changed,' said Sidonie. 'No one smokes here under any circumstances, and that's that. Or there'll be no trip to Barcelona and I'll pack you off to Aunt Edwige's instead.'

Emma got up from the sofa and headed for her room, muttering that she was living under a dictatorship.

That Emma should be called to account over her appearance and her cigarette consumption by Sidonie seemed perfectly reasonable. But I could see that the dictatorship might apply to me too if the effects of the hypnosis began to wear off. The domestic tyranny was going a little too far, a little too quickly, and I needed to ensure I had an escape route.

'You know,' I said, 'we should wait and see. I may not be smoking now, but we can't be sure I won't ever start again.'

'Michel Vaucourt hasn't started again,' said Sidonie immediately.

'I'm not Michel Vaucourt.'

'No, you're Fabrice. And for the moment, you don't smoke. If you feel like smoking again, you'll need to arrange another consultation. I think you look better already,' she added.

I smiled and we poured ourselves another Martini.

'You know, you're a very attractive man, Monsieur Valantine,' she said.

'And you know, if I'd never smoked, we would never have met.'

'To Viktor Frekovitch!' Sidonie raised her glass.

We gazed into one another's eyes for a moment.

'Emma's sleeping over at a friend's place,' she whispered. 'I've arranged a dinner for two.'

The passion sparked by my new status as a non-smoker left me speechless. Sidonie had ordered dinner from Dalloyau. After we had eaten a truffled *feuilleté* and quails in Calvados and drunk a bottle of champagne, my wife asked me – and it sounded like an order – to go to the bathroom and rinse my mouth with Eau de Botot. I did as I was asked, drinking straight from the bottle she had bought for the occasion and diluting it with water from the tap. My smoke-filled years were purged in a baptism of liquorice- and rose-flavoured mouthwash. Sidonie stepped into the room behind me, naked beneath her red and white satin robe. She slipped her hands around my waist and pressed close against my back. I felt the warmth of her body on mine. I reached a hand to her thigh and felt the softness of her skin. She spun me round to face her. Her eyes sparkled as she exclaimed: 'At last, your tongue won't taste like an old ashtray!'

'I tasted like an old ashtray? Why, thank you ...' I replied, somewhat piqued.

'You did,' she said, pushing me towards the bedroom, then slipping off her robe.

The whiteness of her skin, that translucent hue – such a contrast to her jet-black bobbed hair – had always fascinated me. Her full breasts, too, so unexpected for her slender figure.

'How beautiful you are,' I whispered.

I remember that, at that moment, I experienced a feeling of absolute possession. If another man took her away from me one day, I would kill him.

The intoxication of my new-found tobacco sobriety lasted for two weeks. Which is a very long time for a smoker. Two whole weeks. I retain a curious memory of those tobacco-free days, as if they were lived by someone else. I was no longer the same Fabrice Valantine, but a kind of non-smoking doppelgänger.

I did not tell anyone at the office that I had given up. The very next day, I waited to hear the magic words: 'Fabrice, you're not smoking!' I had already practised the deprecating little smile I would give in reply. But the moment never came: to my great astonishment, no one noticed I was no longer smoking. Not Gold, nor Véronique, still less Jean Verider, who nurtured a lifelong addiction to Vichy Pastilles. Everyone was in low spirits. The HBC board was planning for Hubert Beauchamps-Charellier's exit – he would be retiring at the end of the year. People were coming under pressure and there were rumours of profound changes afoot within the firm. Our competitors were even making noises about a possible takeover, or a brutal power grab.

One afternoon, HBC himself called me into his office. I could only spare him a few moments – I was on my way to the St James Club for a meeting. I often used the discreet, prestigious club for interviews with potential candidates.

'A cigar, Fabrice, dear boy?' He opened his sumptuous rose-wood cigar box.

I declined the offer, without going into details. He lit himself a Montecristo No. 1, leaned back in his black leather chair and blew the smoke towards the ceiling. He looked distracted and weary.

'I remember ...' he began, 'when I first called you in here; you were a research assistant, working for Jacquard.'

'I remember that too,' I said. HBC had rung me himself to ask if I had a moment to come up and see him. He had offered me a cigar then, too, and I had declined. I always declined his offers of cigars. 'Are you tempted by the chase, young man? Do you like hunting?' I didn't understand his question or, rather, I didn't dare take his meaning. 'I've never been out shooting,' I replied. He laughed. 'I'm not talking about ducks, Valantine, I mean going after talent – headhunting! I've heard excellent things about you. I'm offering you a new job, an office, a direct line. I want you to become a headhunter.'

Twenty-two years later, neither of us needed to share the memory aloud. We mulled it over in companionable silence.

'I'm leaving, Fabrice. I've done my time.'

'Are you sure?'

He gave a small, sad smile and stared up at the ceiling.

'I want you to take my place.'

I stared at him, and he looked me in the eye. We stayed like that for a few seconds. They seemed like hours to me.

'You must be aware that once I've left there will be jostling for position. That's what I want to avoid. I don't want this marvellous machine I've built to lose its soul.'

'But why me? Why not Gold or Verider?'

'Because you're the best, in my view. You know all the workings of the business; you've been here the longest. You've spent your entire career under one roof. A rare thing nowadays. That's an asset.'

There was nothing I could say.

'Don't thank me,' he said, before I could. 'Trust me. Trust yourself. That's all I ask.'

My phone rang in my pocket. I silenced it hurriedly.

'A meeting?'

'Yes.'

'You still use the St James?'

'I still do, yes.'

'A fine club. Don't make yourself late, we can talk again another time. Not a word until then,' he said, putting a finger to his lips.

We shook hands at length. I was moved, and surprised. In truth, I was realising a dream I had never dared admit: I would be taking the helm at HBC Consulting. The crowning accomplishment of a perfect self-made career. I had come in at the bottom, as a humble assistant, and I would rise to the top of the firm. From the basement to the top floor. Twenty-five years of my life had gone by along the way.

It had begun to rain, and I had left my umbrella at the office. The taxi dropped me just outside the entrance so that I wouldn't get soaked. But in the courtyard, I felt the urge to put down my briefcase, spread my arms wide, throw my head back and feel the raindrops on my face. I wanted to stay there under the rain-soaked sky and think of nothing but the sunlit future that was promised to me now. But I decided against such a theatrical gesture and hurried briskly in through the door.

'How are you today, Jean?' I asked the concierge as he took my raincoat.

'Your table's ready, Monsieur Valantine.'

I headed for the vast panelled room and settled myself into the leather Chesterfield banquette next to the window. Facing me, an armchair in the same style would shortly be occupied by my candidate. It's a tradition that has lapsed lately – arranging a first meeting with a candidate outside the office. But I remain a fierce advocate of this approach. In a place like this, there are no telephones ringing in the background, no wheezing photo-copiers, no conversations behind partition screens nearby. The address should be carefully chosen: neither too luxurious, nor too ordinary, nor too conventional, nor too informal. It should be a place where you can converse at ease and order refreshments as required, in a hushed atmosphere. The St James Club fulfilled all the criteria.

I opened my folder and read through my target candidate's

file one last time. Franck Faye, finance director with Frelia, a Canadian firm specialising in the bottling of fine liqueurs and the packaging of miniatures for the bars and minibars of luxury hotels. Their clients included the major international chains: Hilton, Sheraton, Sofitel, and all the best-known palace hotels. Faye had run the Asian subsidiary, based out of Shanghai, for four years. During this time, Frelia's sales had soared in the region, with annual growth of more than twenty per cent. Another trump card: he spoke fluent Mandarin and understood Cantonese. Chinese wife. Age: thirty-eight. Graduate of a leading Paris university, with that essential ticket to a fast-track career: an MBA from Princeton. Annual salary: a hundred and fifty thousand euros, plus bonuses. Activities and interests: making remote-controlled models. To my mind, he was the perfect fit for Kerko, the American boiled-sweet multinational. The cream of Kerko France and Kerko Belgium had been transferred to Beijing for the opening of a Kerko subsidiary in Asia. As I understood it, a family dispute had led to the departure of their finance director, and the manager they had put in his place was proving unsuitable. News of a vacancy had reached me through an informant at Kerko France, whom I had recruited two years previously. He had provided me with regular snippets ever since, like most of my former candidates. Another tradition in our business, which some hypocrites honour only in the form of a seasonal greetings card once a year. When the formal request landed on my desk, I had immediately thought of the approach I had received by email the week before. Franck Faye had sent me his CV on the advice of a friend I had headhunted six months earlier. He wanted a settled position in China for the next five years. A move from Frelia Shanghai to Kerko Beijing was a possibility.

'Fabrice Valantine?'

I looked up. White-blond hair, pale complexion, a round face, gold-framed glasses and a broad smile. He looked younger than thirty-eight. I got to my feet and shook his hand. Firm grip. A highly approachable, pleasant man. I noticed the small creases around his eyes that made him look as if he was always in a good mood. He ordered a tomato juice. Perrier with lemon for me. We began by talking about vegetables. Conversations often start with subjects far removed from the one we are there to discuss. I discovered that his wife gave cookery classes on an Asian TV channel, and that she was the author of a book of juiced vegetable recipes that was selling out fast in Shanghai. I also learned that his blond hair came from his mother, who was Swedish. Lastly, I learned that he was very familiar with Kerko's product range, and that he had met one of their directors on a flight from Paris to New York: both were passionate about model-making and happened to be reading the same brochure advertising the latest miniature aeroplanes. He was ideal. A dream candidate: the kind you hope to meet at every interview. After examining his career in detail and discussing his salary requirements – a rising curve, obviously – he asked my permission to smoke while enjoying a second tomato juice.

'I don't smoke at the office. Just a few a day, at the right time.'

'I know exactly what you mean ... I've given up. Well, I think I have,' I added.

'Well done. Do you use a substitute?'

'No, you'll laugh when I tell you ...'

At last, a chance to use my studied smile, as yet uncalled-for at HBC.

'I went to a hypnotist.'

'Really? Amazing ... Apparently, it works.'

'Apparently. My wife talked me into it.'

'Always listen to your wife!' he concluded, with the same boyish grin.

The conversation could have carried on in this vein for a good twenty minutes had my phone not rung.

The name, GOLD came up on the screen. Which was odd. He seldom called me on my mobile and would normally check with Sabine first to see if I was in a meeting. I took the call.

'It's Gold. Are you still in your meeting?'

'Yes,' I said. 'Is something the matter?'

'Can you come back to the office afterwards?'

'I wasn't planning to, but yes, I can. What's happened?'

'HBC is dead.'

The information took a few seconds to sink in. *HBC is dead.* As a kind of reflex, I told him it wasn't possible, I'd been talking to him an hour ago. Gold told me he'd been dead just fifteen minutes, and that Sabine had found him sprawled on the carpet. He was gone in seconds, a massive heart attack.

'His cigar burned a hole in the carpet,' he added.

I heard him swallow.

'*Voilà*,' he said finally, his voice cracking.

'I'm on my way,' I muttered weakly, before snapping my phone shut.

I looked across at Franck Faye, but realised I couldn't see him. A film of tears blurred my vision.

'Let's cut short our meeting, Monsieur Valantine,' he said gravely.

'Yes. It's not a family matter ... Hubert Beauchamps-Charellier has died. *Voilà*.' My voice was cracking now.

He nodded solemnly and spoke a few perfectly chosen words: 'I understand. He was an iconic figure in your profession.'

'Absolutely. Iconic,' I repeated dully.

At that moment, I realised that an essential part of my past had disappeared in a matter of seconds, like a section of ice that splits off from an iceberg and sinks without trace beneath the half-frozen waves. A tearing and crashing then nothing. The dark, liquid deep. My sense of bereavement over the loss of my cigarettes was coupled now with my very real mourning for HBC. What would I do without my cigarettes and now without HBC, who watched over us all like a patriarch and protector?

The man I was two weeks ago had suffered a profound change. In herpetology, the species would be said to have undergone metamorphosis, combined with alterations in its habitat. Which posed the fundamental question: how would the species survive?

HBC's death called into question our last conversation in his office. He'd had no time to organise a formal succession. I had enough experience of our business to know that a man's word is worth nothing unless it's written down in black and white and signed by both parties. There's little to say about my return to the office and the evening I spent with Sidonie. She was kind enough to insist I could still rise to the top of the firm. I don't know whether she said it to please me, but I didn't believe it would happen now.

Scenes from my twenty-five years at HBC came back to me. I saw Hubert Beauchamps-Charellier, Montecristo in hand. I owed my career to that man, with his ability to sniff out the best Havana cigars and the best candidates. An anecdote sprang to mind. A bittersweet anecdote, I admit, but it raised a smile that evening.

Fifteen years earlier, a new assistant who, despite being sweet-natured, could also be fiery, had received a telling-off. HBC had totally lost his usual composure: the young woman must have stood up to him in no uncertain terms for him to lose his temper so completely. Véronique Beauffancourt and I were passing in the corridor and stopped on hearing raised voices from his office. The young assistant had flung the door wide open at that moment.

'Come back here this minute, Mademoiselle!' HBC had thundered.

But she had gathered up her things and was already stuffing them into her bag.

'No way!' she had yelled. 'I'm not going to let some old queer tell me what to do!'

HBC was out of his chair. He appeared in the doorway with a stricken expression. The little pest had dared to say out loud what everyone in the office knew but never mentioned: HBC was unmarried and childless ... A confirmed bachelor of fifty-eight, and obviously gay. A taboo subject in the firm, unmentionable even under torture. He looked in our direction, then along the corridor at the retreating assistant. His face darkened. Pointing after her, he boomed: 'That, Mademoiselle, is an insult too far. Queer, absolutely. Old, never!' And with that, he had disappeared back into his office, slamming the door behind him.

HBC's spirited retort reverberated in the darkening sitting room. In the space of two weeks, I had lost my cigarettes, I had lost HBC, and I had lost the spectacular promotion he had offered me on the very day of his death. I couldn't bring HBC or my promotion back. But one thing was in my power. I could put my hand into my jacket pocket, take out my packet of cigarettes and light up. I had smoked so many cigarettes for no good reason that this one seemed more than deserved. There's no harm in smoking just this one, I told myself, rolling it between my fingers. Perhaps from now on, I can limit myself to just a few a day. It reassured me to think that this familiar act would remain with me, at least. Sidonie wouldn't like it, of course, but she wouldn't object to it this evening: I had lost my boss, and my prospect of promotion. Enough for one day. I could hear her talking in English from the bedroom. She would be taking advantage of the time difference to call the States.

To mark the occasion, I took a gold-plated Zippo lighter out of the drawer. The flint sparked and I had had the good sense to leave a little bottle of fuel beside it. I poured the oily liquid onto the cotton, clicked the lighter and watched as the flame flared for an instant in the palm of my hand before dying back and cleaving to the wick. I shut the lid with a sharp snap, then opened it again immediately. Click. I held the flame to my cigarette. Sitting on the sofa, I would allow myself a few minutes of thoroughly deserved relaxation. The cigarette would lift my spirits as surely as any antidepressant. At the tip, the small circle of tobacco glowed. I closed the lighter and took my first drag. After two weeks of abstinence, the cigarette was sure to set my head spinning. Its effect would be stronger than ever.

The smoke went in and out of my lungs.

Nothing.

I tried again.

Nothing.

I felt no more pleasure than I did breathing in air. I took another drag. I would feel the tingle, the soothing effect of the nicotine as it relaxed my muscles and brain.

But I didn't.

Nothing, absolutely nothing, happened.

Seized with panic, I took the cigarette out of my mouth and examined it as if it might be faulty. But no, it was perfectly normal, identical to its umpteen thousand siblings I had smoked since I was seventeen. I took another drag and blew out the smoke. Nothing.

Perhaps it wasn't the cigarette – perhaps it was me. I remembered the bloated face of the large man on the café terrace in Place des Abbesses, with his finger pointing at his forehead. 'It's all in your head,' he had said. What was going on in there? What had the hypnotist blocked in my brain so that I no longer felt any pleasure in smoking?

I felt the urge for a second cigarette and lit one straight away. The urge had returned, but not the pleasure. Not the desired effect. No joy. No relaxation. Nothing.

Nothing at all.

It begins with an airless labyrinth, suffocatingly hot. The soft, shiny, plastic walls are bathed in pink light. I feel small, warm, trembling bodies all around me. I am one of them. Some kind of starting signal must have been given, but I have heard nothing. We all scurry along the narrow corridor. To my great astonishment, I'm a white mouse, covered in sleek, silky fur, exactly like all the others racing alongside me. I recognise Jean Gold, he's a mouse too, smoking his Dunhill pipe. Véronique Beauffancourt has a Vogue cigarette clenched between her teeth. A mouse bigger than the rest pushes through the crowd, smoking a cigar. I recognise HBC. Turning a corner in the corridor, we come across another mouse, with a giant Vichy mint on its back, crying out: 'I'll never go to the canteen again!' I recognise Jean Verider. I want to ask Gold what we're all doing inside the labyrinth. Strangely, it's not being a mouse that bothers me most, but the unfamiliar setting. Galloping along, I find myself beside Véronique, who tells me to hurry up or 'there'll be none left'. The phrase stresses me still further. Next, we pass into a narrow tube, one at a time. The tube opens onto a huge, transparent slope, down which we all slide: we are in a Plexiglas pipe, like a slide in an aqua-park. But there's no water. We slide down the pipe and our little claws scrape the sides. The falling sensation frightens me. We end up in a bar with a copper-topped counter, so highly polished I can see my face in it, like a golden mirror. I recognise my little pink nose straight away. The other mice jostle me, slipping and sliding on the metal surface. Everyone hurries towards a device at the end of the counter. A kind of peanut dispenser, the sort they used to have in the sixties. I notice that Gold has lost his pipe, Véronique no longer has her Vogue cigarette, and HBC is minus his cigar. I'm patting my fur, looking for my packet of Benson & Hedges, but I can't find it. Gold is the first to reach the device. He presses a small pedal and strains his head towards the flap. A flurry of nuts strikes his nose. Véronique pushes him aside and activates the pedal in turn. Another flurry of nuts. It's my turn. I press the pedal but nothing comes out. I try again. Nothing. The container is empty. I feel desperately anxious. I turn to the rest of the room. My mousey friends have assumed human form once more. The bar resembles an English club, with soft lighting and black walls. Everyone is talking and smoking. Some are lounging in deep club sofas, others are leaning against the walls. I recognise Gold in the crowd, talking to another pipe smoker. I've seen the man some-where before; he's quite elderly, with glasses, and an odd-looking bootlace tie. I remember his name: it's Georges Simenon. Just behind him, Winston Churchill is wearing a big sailor's cap, chewing on half a cigar and holding a bottle of whisky in one hand. Véronique is chatting to a man in faded jeans, whose face I can't make out. He seizes her by the neck. I see a packet of Gitanes in his right hand. He tries to kiss her, and I recognise Serge Gainsbourg. Looking around, I see Hubert Beauchamps-Charellier asking Sacha Guitry for a light. 'Of course, with pleasure,' replies the actor. I see his hands with astonishing clarity: his nails are quite long, and his immaculate white cuffs are fastened with diamond cufflinks bearing his initials. He clicks a Dupont lighter and lights HBC's cigar. Behind them, Humphrey Bogart is accompanied by a very beautiful blonde woman with an outsize cigarette holder. I want desperately to join them; I turn back to the nut dispenser and press the pedal twenty times or more with my paw, but nothing comes out.

'Oh no! No – not here!' Sacha Guitry's voice comes from just behind me. He's huge. He grabs me by the tail; I feel myself being lifted into the air, and I see the whole room upside down. 'Look who's here!' he exclaims.

I thrash the air with my little paws. I try to turn myself the right way up, but to no avail. Guitry carries me over to a woman's cleavage and drops me down into it. To my surprise, she doesn't react. I can't see a thing: I'm stuck between her breasts. Suddenly, the light becomes very bright and I'm walking over her sunlit skin, pink like the corridor where it all began.

I recognise these breasts – they belong to Sidonie. I feel immensely relieved, and calm. She alone can tell me why the little nut dispenser didn't work for me. I'm about to walk up her neck and ask her, when I wake with a start.

I had this dream several times during my two-week abstinence from cigarettes. I know exactly what prompted it: an article in the 'Science and Medicine' section of a magazine I had read at work: 'Smokers Powerless to Fight Dependency'.

The article stated that researchers at the Institut Pasteur and other French research centres had collaborated with their Swedish counterparts to analyse the subtle correlations between the different types of nicotine receptor in the brain. It seemed that their work, published in distinguished scientific reviews, might well lead to the development of therapeutic drugs capable of breaking nicotine dependency.

The researchers had succeeded in isolating specific neurones where specialist receptors were located. The latter functioned like microscopic locks that fitted together, binding with inhaled nicotine. Nine sub-units had been identified, known as 'alphas', together with three 'betas', all of which could combine on the surface of the neurones to form hundreds of nicotine receptors. This sophisticated alchemy all took place in a precisely defined section of the brain: the ventral tegmental area or VTA, the locus for a range of dependencies, including nicotine. The scientists had bred a genetically programmed mouse whose nicotine receptors were missing the beta 2 sub-unit. The mouse stubbornly refused to overdose on nicotine, while the other 'normal' mice – when placed in the presence of a nicotine spray and a pedal to activate it – became addicted in no time at all and pressed the pedal all day long to get their fix.

The same singularly motivated team had also deciphered what they termed the molecular foundations of our 'reward system' – the system that plays a central role in drug dependency. When we smoke a cigarette, the nicotine receptors in our brain are activated, the carrier neurones are stimulated, and we feel pleasure.

And what had happened in my case? The urge to smoke had returned, but the pleasure had vanished. I didn't deserve such punishment. Which alpha or beta molecule had become blocked in my brain? I was a frigid tobaccomaniac. I invented the term one afternoon and wrote it down on my notepad before tearing the sheet out and throwing it furiously into the waste-paper basket. I should never have set foot in the consulting room of that hypnotist. He had been the catalyst for this disaster. It had been one of those encounters that seem to jinx everything so that you wonder what you've done to deserve it. Marco Di Caro was responsible for everything, even Hubert Beauchamps-Charellier's death. That man had altered my destiny. I had to erase what he had done: I had to contact him once again and persuade him to reverse the process.

One Saturday morning, I went back to Rue Lamarck. Two days before, I had booked another appointment with Di Caro by telephone. This time, I made the call myself.

'Was your last session unsuccessful?' he asked, anxiously.

'It's a little more complicated than that,' I replied. 'I'll explain on Saturday.'

I had relived the previous session in my mind and decided that once I arrived outside Di Caro's building, I would look at myself in the brass plate and take a long drag on a cigarette before discarding the stub and heading through the door. The thought of this ritual magic reassured me. This second session would be a perfect rerun of the first, but with the exact opposite aim: I would become a smoker again, as if nothing had happened.

I had imagined that Di Caro might refuse, pleading God knows what professional ethic, and I had armed myself with a fat wad of cash, confident that he would be unlikely to refuse that, at least. I spent the intervening days in a state of outright panic. My fragile internal compass had been thrown completely off-kilter, but I confessed my troubles to no one. How could I explain that smoking brought me no pleasure and that this discovery had plunged me into the abyss? I couldn't bother Gold and Véronique with it; they hadn't even noticed I had given up. And I could confide still less in Sidonie, who, as a non-smoker, was clearly proud of my recent efforts.

As soon as I turned onto Rue Caulaincourt, I saw something

was wrong. Outside Di Caro's building, a police van and two unmarked cars were parked at an angle on the pavement. As I approached, Di Caro appeared in the doorway, flanked by two men who led him to the van. One of them was speaking into his mouthpiece; the other wore mirrored shades and chewed on a piece of gum. I hurried towards Di Caro. We exchanged looks just before he climbed into the police vehicle. And that was all. The men slammed the doors shut. Two uniformed officers emerged from the parked cars and requested instructions from the man with the mirrored shades, who whispered to them before slapping the van twice with the palm of his hand. The engine started and it pulled out into the traffic.

I walked up to the men and saw my distorted reflection in the police officer's mirrored Ray-Ban Aviators.

'Excuse me for asking,' I said, 'but I had an appointment with the man you've just taken away.'

'Really?' he said. 'Looks like he's going to be fully booked for the next two or three years.'

'I don't understand.'

'You saw what just happened – it's called an arrest, Monsieur,' he said drily.

His phone rang and he moved away to take the call. The only words I managed to hear were 'Our investigation is underway.'

While his back was turned, I slipped inside the building through the wide-open door. I had no idea what I hoped to achieve. I probably wanted to go through with the scenario I had planned in my head: climb the stairs to the sixth floor and stand in front of the hypnotist's door. I had played the scene over and over in my mind that day, and couldn't imagine not seeing it through. I bounded up the stairs to Di Caro's consulting room, taking them four at a time. The door stood open. Quietly, I stepped forward. Two men of about thirty, one with brown hair, the other with a completely shaved head, were moving along the hallway, talking. On the chest of drawers, I recognised the card with the small printed hand pointing to the waiting room on the left.

'Excuse me, gentlemen,' I called out, knocking on the open door. They turned to look at me.

'I have an appointment with Monsieur Di Caro,' I said, in all innocence.

Far from the dry irony of his colleague downstairs, the thirty-year-old with the shaved head gave an apologetic smile.

'Bad timing,' he said, pretending to consult his watch. 'Did you know him?'

'Yes. Well, I met him once – I came for hypnosis, and I wanted to see him again.'

He nodded.

'See that?' he addressed his colleague. 'That was the genius of the operation. The perfect cover. There'll be loads of people like this man here. Ten, a hundred, a thousand? Who knows. Anything's possible. Say what you like.'

'You're right, Lieutenant,' the other man nodded.

The bald man shifted his gaze back to me.

'So you were one of his clients, were you? Come in. Lieutenant Masquettier,' he introduced himself, shaking me by the hand.

'Fabrice Valantine.'

I entered the hypnotist's waiting room, as before. Everything was exactly as I had pictured it would be, except that Di Caro was no longer there and I was talking to the police.

'May I ask what you do for a living?' said the lieutenant.

He seemed like a pleasant enough type. He glided rather oddly around the room, as if conscious of his tall, thin frame.

'I'm a headhunter.'

He looked impressed, just as Di Caro had.

'That's a job I'd have liked to do,' he said. 'It was my second choice if the police force didn't work out.'

I responded with a small friendly smile.

'Who are you with?' he asked.

'HBC Consulting.'

'Best in the business,' he said.

I saw a brief glimmer of regret in his eyes, a kind of nostalgia for what might have been, for the path not taken. He looked at the sheaf of blue papers marked 'WHY HYPNOSIS?', took one of the sheets and glanced through it.

'So what was your craving?' he asked.

'Smoking.'

'And he cured you?'

'Not really.'

'Doesn't surprise me. If Di Caro's a hypnotist, then I'm the Pope.'

His words hit me like a blow. I stared at him, transfixed. What had he just said? It wasn't possible; I must have misunderstood. And yet, I had understood him perfectly.

The revelation of my line of business prompted revelations of his own. Di Caro was a small cog in a much bigger money-laundering machine. His real name was Jacques Poliveau. The highly organised network involved fake mediums, clairvoyants, tarot readers and hypnotists. None required any sort of qualification to practise and, above all, they demanded payment in cash. Di Caro and others were used to launder dirty money from drugs, racketeering and prostitution, after which the sums reappeared, perfectly legally, as false tax returns, none of which could be checked. The network covered a wide area and significant sums were involved. The anti-money-laundering department at the Ministry of Finance had been working with the police for a year and a half to bring the scam to light. According to the lieutenant, the system involved far more than the twenty individuals arrested that morning in Paris – it reached right across France. Millions of euros were being moved around by thousands of people.

'It's a pyramid laundering scam: your hypnotist and the others are the base. You trace it back from there. Catch one and they all go down like dominoes.'

I was completely uninterested in money-laundering systems, fake tax returns and the cash economy. All that mattered to me was the words 'If Di Caro's a hypnotist, then I'm the Pope.'

'So he was never a hypnotist?'

Stupidly, helplessly, I repeated the question. I needed to hear it said again. I was almost on the point of asking him to write it down in black and white, sign it and certify it with a rubber stamp.

'Never!'

And yet Michel Vaucourt had stopped smoking and a client of Michel Vaucourt's had stopped, too. As for me, I had a mental block. I told the lieutenant about Michel Vaucourt. He shrugged. It was definitely 'something psychological', he said, a little like the placebo effect, which was well documented for medicines. Our conversation was halted when a young man in jeans entered the room carrying Di Caro's computer. He swore and complained that it was heavy; he should have help for this sort of thing: he was a software expert, not a removals guy. A brief, slightly tense exchange ended in a volley of colourful jokes.

'Thank you, Monsieur, and goodbye,' said the lieutenant pleasantly, indicating that our interview was at an end. He told me I should file a complaint against Di Caro.

A complaint about what? The two hundred euros my session had cost me? I wasn't bothered about that in the least. About losing all pleasure in smoking? No complaint procedure would take a claim of that sort into consideration. I pictured myself giving evidence in the non-smoking offices of some public administration, explaining that nicotine no longer had any effect on my brain's pleasure centre, or reward system, which was itself governed by endorphins; or perhaps drawing blackboard diagrams of my alphas and betas, and cross-sections of my brain and lungs, before a dazed audience. Ludicrous. Impossible. A complete dead end. There was no form of complaint in existence for the crime of entering and breaking your victim's brain.

When I emerged from the building, the man in the mirrored shades shot me a dark look and stared after me as I walked off towards Place des Abbesses. I wanted to leave Sidonie a message, to tell her that Di Caro was no hypnotist, that he was a crook wanted by the police, that his supposed 'gifts' were a cover, nothing more, and that Michel Vaucourt had been conned along with all the others, not forgetting those on whom his fake hypnosis sessions had had no effect whatsoever, and who certainly wouldn't be boasting about losing their two hundred euros. The script of my angry phone call was so perfect that I decided not to make it. I've often noticed that if an interview or a presentation is over-prepared, it becomes meaningless: you reach the meeting or the seminar podium and freeze. The rehearsal has used up your creative energy.

Emerging from this train of thought, I realised that I had walked around the block three times in succession. I decided to wander the streets at random, in an effort to calm myself. My steps took me to the window of the bric-a-brac shop with its ashtrays advertising vintage tobacco brands. None had been bought. Was there no nostalgia for tobacco? I pushed the door, and the bell tinkled. Five minutes later, I left the shop carrying a heavy plastic bag: I had bought the lot, at too high a price, no doubt, but the cash I had brought along for Di Caro was burning a hole in my pocket and I had to get rid of it. The shop's owner had wrapped everything in bubble wrap; the bag was bulging and the handles cut into my fingers. I decided to make for the café where I had met the large cigar smoker. He was there again, still with his phone pressed to his ear. I sat down a few tables away. He recognised me and gave a barely perceptible sign of greeting.

I placed the heavy bag on the chair next to mine. What would I order? The morning's events called for something completely unexpected, it seemed to me, and when the waiter approached, I asked for a Viandox. In the middle of May. While waiting for my steaming bowl of beef broth, I scrutinised the large man as he pulled from his pocket a cigar case divided into three compartments. He extracted a Romeo y Julieta, placed it between his teeth, struck a match and began to warm the foot, in a smooth, practised sequence of gestures. Instinctively, I reached for my packet of Benson & Hedges and placed it on the table with my Bic lighter. I watched him resentfully: the urge, but not the pleasure. Lighting up would produce no more effect than if I were to breathe the polluted air of the street. A puff of cigar smoke wafted over my face, then another. And another. Cigar smokers need to take several puffs in quick succession to ensure an even light. I knew the ritual.

The man hadn't spoken a word. I wondered if there was really someone on the other end of his call. I noted his appearance: elegantly dressed, with the brick-red complexion of a whisky drinker, grey-white hair worn longish and slicked back, a thick, bull-like neck. Difficult to determine his age. It was strange to find him still there. He might almost have been waiting for me. An absurd thought struck me. What if this big man was really here just for me? What if he was an emissary of the Devil, or even the Devil himself?

The waiter put my bowl of Viandox down on the table, slipped the bill into the saucer and walked away. The large man hailed him as he passed.

'Another,' he said, pointing to his glass.

Then he turned to me.

'Remember me?' I asked him.

'Of course. You're the fake smoker. So, is the hypnosis working?'

'Not really.'

The curious idea that this man was not entirely real was taking hold. I could be utterly frank with him. It didn't matter.

'The man I saw wasn't a hypnotist; in fact, he was a crook. The police have just taken him away.'

'Haha! That's a good one!' He laughed heartily as he removed his cigar from his mouth and blew on the tip.

'Unfortunately, something did work even if he was play-acting,' I went on, gravely. 'I get no pleasure from smoking any more.'

'Really?'

'Really,' I sighed, bending over my steaming bowl of broth.

With his cigar in his hand, the man looked over at the buildings across the street, then addressed me in confidential tones: 'If I got no pleasure from smoking, I'd hang myself.'

'But that still leaves red wine and rare-cooked roast lamb,' I reminded him.

He stifled a small laugh.

'I'd give twenty legs of lamb for one of these,' he said, brandishing his cigar.

The waiter delivered his tumbler of whisky and he sipped at it. I waited for my Viandox to cool and took one of the ashtrays out of its bubble wrapping. Cléopâtre, a triangular model with Egyptian motifs, for a brand of cigarettes that had long since disappeared. The object caught my neighbour's attention. Moments later, I handed him a different one, then another. He was delighted by the collection. He had smoked some of these brands, he told me, which left me still more perplexed as to his age. I watched as he marvelled at the old ashtrays and an idea came to me.

'You can have them all,' I said.

He looked up. He was suspicious now, on the defensive. I could tell, and he quickly confirmed it. There was no such thing as a free gift, he said. His business career had taught him that. A present would always be cashed in sooner or later. So what was I after?

'Your employee. The one who practises hypnosis,' I said. 'I want to meet him.'

Sidonie refused to believe me. She made me tell her the story of my visit to the hypnotist and my conversation with the police lieutenant several times over before she would admit that Di Caro was indeed a crook. The fact that I had lost all pleasure in smoking, which I eventually confided to her, was completely eclipsed by my revelation of the man's true identity as a charlatan. That same evening, she called Michel Vaucourt's wife to tell her the unexpected news. She, in turn, immediately told Vaucourt.

My one ray of sunshine in those dire weeks was this: incredulous at first, Michel Vaucourt had called a magistrate friend who, after making a few enquiries, confirmed that a massive anti-money-laundering operation had indeed taken place in Paris, and that one of the men arrested was indeed Jacques Poliveau, better known as Marco Di Caro. Astounded, Michel Vaucourt had taken up smoking again that same evening. I was delighted to hear of his capitulation. But my joy was short-lived: my interview with the cigar smoker's employee would leave me still more deeply perplexed.

Four o'clock in the morning. I had set my phone to vibrate, so as not to wake Sidonie. I told her I had found contact details for another hypnotist, but a real one this time; he was a porter at Rungis wholesale market, just south of Paris, and I would have to go there to meet him. But I lied about the true reason for our dawn assignation. I did not tell Sidonie that I would be asking him to reverse what Di Caro had done. No: as far as Sidonie was concerned, our meeting was arranged so that he could finish what Di Caro had started.

Stiff from lack of sleep, and yawning at the wheel of my car, I narrowly avoided an accident on my way to Rungis. Once there, I wandered through the vast hangars, lined with pallets of fruit and vegetables as far as the eye could see. Porters stacked great piles of them one on top of the other, as if trying to construct a new Tower of Babel entirely out of boxes of vegetables. The hangars at Rungis were only the foundations, other levels would soon be added, the structure would be gargantuan, with its head in the clouds, the food of all mankind piled up to heaven. I despaired of finding Manu, the cigar man's employee, when my phone rang. It was him. My number was registered in his call history from the call I had made the night before. When I failed to appear, he had had the good sense to phone me.

'Where are you?'

'I don't know.'

'What can you see?'

'Melons. Hundreds of melons.'

'Go straight on to shallots, first left, oranges and nectarines, then straight ahead. I'm in the strawberries.'

Following his directions, I came upon him behind a mountain of strawberry punnets. A young man of no more than twenty, with a long ponytail down his back. Notebook in hand, he was counting and recounting his deliveries. He gave a broad smile and extended a soft, limp hand.

'You're a friend of Monsieur Doppio?'

I had learned the cigar man's name. He hadn't given it and I hadn't thought to ask.

'Not really. Let's just say I made his acquaintance and he told me about your gift,' I said.

The young man gave an embarrassed laugh. He was clearly very shy. I told him about my strange mental block and my wish to get rid of it. Around us, the strawberry punnets gave off a sweet, almost intoxicating smell. He put down his notebook and pen, invited me politely to sit on a big wooden chest, checked I could lean back against the punnets without staining my clothes or crushing the fruit, then took a step back and stared into my eyes. His features altered. The veneer of shyness disappeared. He held a hand in front of my forehead and intoned: 'Here and now, you are going to fall deeply asleep, you're sleeping, sleeping ...'

He placed his hand between my eyebrows, the red strawberries grew blurry, and I lost consciousness.

'Four, three, two, one, zero. You're waking up.'

I opened my eyes. The young man was looking at me, perplexed.

'You've got a complete mental block,' he said.

He went on to tell me that I had said nothing at all about my need to smoke. Quite the opposite, I had clammed up like an oyster, to use his expression, as soon as he tried to broach the subject. In my sleep phase, I had claimed not to remember my first cigarette, nor that my parents had been smokers, nor even to know any other smokers. I had admitted to smoking, however, but had said nothing further on the subject. What did surprise him was that I had talked about Sidonie, quite unprompted.

'You must love your wife very much,' he said, in a concerned tone. 'Excuse me for asking, but ... are you quite jealous?'

'Jealous? Me? Not at all.'

'Strange,' he murmured.

He moved on to my problem with cigarettes – the reason for my visit. According to him, Di Caro wasn't entirely a charlatan.

He had managed to put me to sleep, so he must have some basic knowledge of hypnosis. Only the rudiments, he thought, but enough to induce the sleep stage. What had he done while I was under? That was the question. My brain was like the workings of a Rolex watch, said this likeable young man. The idea came to him when he spotted the model I was wearing on my wrist. He reminded me of something I had forgotten about the famous brand: only Rolex-approved watchmakers are allowed to open and repair them, though that doesn't stop others from trying. But if a problem occurs as a result of an unskilled, unofficial repair job, Rolex will refuse to touch the piece again.

'I'm Rolex, do you see what I mean? I have no idea what he did in there,' he said, pointing to my forehead, 'so I can't do anything. You should have come to me first, not the watchmaker round the corner.'

'So what can be done?'

'The only person who can do anything about it is the same watchmaker round the corner.'

Manu refused to take any money. He didn't do it for the money. Besides which, he said he hadn't done anything anyway. His watchmaking metaphor left me stranded down one of the biggest dead ends of my life. I thought about going back to the police, getting in touch with Di Caro's lawyer and demanding a visit, just long enough for a hypnosis session. The ideas swirling in my head hit a solid wall of absurdity: in the eyes of all concerned, I would look like a harmless nutcase at best and, at worst, like someone in the grip of a full-blown manic episode. I faced these painful hours with no solace whatsoever, just the dusty taste of my cigarettes and the utter ineffectiveness of the nicotine.

There's a dynamic of success, and a dynamic of failure, too. I thought I had hit rock bottom when my delight in smoking disappeared. But I was wrong. I had further to go. The beautiful shiny bow on the gift box of my rise to the summit of HBC Consulting had come undone and the contents were tainted with poison. Like some latterday Christ on the road to Calvary, I staggered under the weight of a gigantic cigarette. Soon, I would come before my very own Pontius Pilate, in the person of Franck Louvier.

The manoeuvring that Hubert Beauchamps-Charellier had feared, came to pass. The board took everyone by surprise and appointed a newcomer to the top job: a renegade they had head-hunted themselves, in what they hoped was a fine display of dynamism and initiative. HBC Consulting had been managed by the same group of people for a very long time, and perhaps they wanted to signal a change of style. Franck Louvier was a prodigal son of France, Harvard-trained, who had enjoyed swash-buckling success in a string of stock-market operations and IPOs before joining one of the big names in consultancy. Blond, with a decidedly short Stateside haircut and pale wolf-like eyes, the youthful forty-one-year-old made his entrance one morning and launched straight into a tour of the offices, escorted by a couple of yes-men. He shook everyone by the hand, from the department heads down to the interns, then invited us all to join him in the conference room on the second floor. My initial contact with him was brief. Brief and detestable. He opened my office door without knocking, to find me deep in research behind my computer screen, while a cigarette burned in my ashtray. I hadn't attempted to smoke it: it was just burning, solitary and useless, like an incense stick lit in honour of some long-departed god.

'Hello Fabrice. Franck Louvier,' he introduced himself, crushing my hand. 'The offices are strictly non-smoking. See you in the executive space at three.'

And with that he left.

I hadn't had time to so much as open my mouth. I stared at the door, which was closed again now. He had referred to the conference room as the 'executive space'. Cretin. No one ever called the conference room anything of the kind. It was the 'purple room', a reference to the colour of the curtains at the tall windows a long time ago. The elder statesmen of HBC were the only ones who remembered them, but the name had stuck. At three o'clock we gathered in the purple room and waited for the address from our new head. I sat between Gold and Jean Verider. Véronique had been dispatched to London to meet a potential candidate.

'He caught me with my pipe,' confided Gold.

'Same here, I had a lit cigarette in my ashtray,' I replied.

'He told me I should lose some weight,' said Verider, indignantly, chomping nervously on a Vichy Pastille. 'He came in, *winked* at me, and said: "You should exercise more; we'll soon shift those kilos …" Well, he can fuck right off, the loser,' he concluded, in outraged tones.

The anointed one arrived ten minutes late. We all noted what we had observed on first contact: Louvier didn't wear a tie. He sported a silvery-grey three-piece suit, but no tie, and the neck of his sky-blue shirt was open.

'Does he even know what a tie is? Jerk …' declared Jean Verider.

'Must be the new fashion,' I ventured.

'He'll ban us all from wearing them before you know it,' said Gold.

We all three glanced down at our respective ties, essential uniform in the service sector, our field of operations. We were at the top of our game, with neckwear to match: Lanvin for me, Hermès for Jean Verider, Versace for Gold. A curious feeling came over me as we sat preening our plumage. Not so much a feeling as a realisation. With our ironic quips and our luxury ties, we represented the Old Guard. We weren't stuck in our ways, but our combined flying hours would count against us from now on. Youthful, thrusting Franck Louvier had one idea in his head: to put the old hunters like us out to grass and stock his stable with younger blood, people like himself. The feeling was confirmed by every word in his pointless speech, full of references to globalisation, the mobile workforce and new technologies. His small tribute to Hubert Beauchamps-Charellier was too short for my liking and demonstrated his complete ignorance of the man, still less his founding philosophy. When he began talking about 'networked individuals as nano-transmitters of the economic metasphere' we exchanged icy looks, in silence.

'In a few days, the departmental directors will each receive a note by email, an opportunity for us all to meet up and get to know one another a little better. I'll say nothing more for now! Good luck to all of you and good luck for the future of this firm: here's to a new world of opportunity! Thank you.'

Dutiful applause greeted the end of the speech.

Jean Gold supplied its fitting conclusion.

'HBC, pray for us ...' he whispered.

On the evening of that dark day, I accompanied the women in my life to the airport. We rode to Orly in a people-carrier taxi. Sidonie was taking flight 675544 to New York; Emma, flight 997261, to Barcelona. Seated beside the driver was Benjamin, Emma's boyfriend, a youth with ambitions to become an author of comic books. I had taken little interest in the doodlings and scribblings of the object of my daughter's affections, but rather more in his family. My paternal question: 'And what do this young man's parents do?' had received a satisfactory response: his father was a big shot in advertising, and his mother was a journalist for *Elle*. We had avoided the worst. The boy's ambitions could have indicated a dubious second-rate artistic milieu: his father a singer of nostalgic rock standards in provincial concert halls, his mother a vaped-out ex-hippy devotee of Hare Krishna and heaven knows what besides. Not so. A point in Benjamin's favour. The boy seemed pleasant enough and well brought up. There was nothing in his appearance or physique that could possibly offend and, yet, I could not help but feel a degree of caution and distrust towards him. Mingled with a touch of dislike. A curious cocktail. One I think every father of a daughter has tasted at least once. Even if our daughters break away from us in adolescence, to an extent, they are forever the children whose outpouring of affection once changed our world. The taxi sped through the dark and I remembered Emma as a little girl, looking at me with her big, adoring eyes; her displays of temper if I refused to pick her up, and so many other moments from that time when I had been her hero. Fathers are unwitting objects of fascination for their daughters, and the interlude of their childhood leaves a bittersweet taste: never again, for anyone else, will we be domestic demi-gods, greeted like long-awaited saviours when we come home for dinner at the end of the working day. The years go by and their joy becomes less and less palpable, until one day they fail to greet us at all. That time has passed, and the countdown reaches zero. We had known it would happen. We just hadn't expected it to happen so quickly.

The taxi sped beneath the repeating light of the lamps on the Périphérique. I would be alone tonight, and for a week, but the prospect was unenticing. I thought of calling Gold to suggest dinner, but decided against it. In our profession, there can be no sign of weakness, still less defeat. If the Old Guard found itself meeting outside work to grumble over *confit de canard*, it would mark the beginning of the end. I would dine alone in front of some rubbish or other on TV. The taxi hummed and the pulse of the street lamps lit Sidonie's face with regular flashes of orange. I studied her profile. Forehead, nose, mouth, upper lip, lower lip, chin, neck. My wife was mysterious, I thought. Enigmatic. The adjective suited her. There was a part of Sidonie that would be forever closed to me, beginning with her profession and the people in it: the art that was as remote to me as fractal equations. Sidonie inhabited her world, and I mine. My world was more real: people came with a price; they were hired for a given time, for their skills, and paid handsomely in exchange. The whole system made the world go round, and created jobs for other people, drawing on their skills in turn. My world was logical. Sidonie's was irrational. Serious, highly serious, but irrational. Artworks were worth more than the men who had created them, often achieving colossal sums of money at sale. A single picture could be worth as much as a small business; one museum's holdings could equate to the GDP of an African state. The galleries played the role of the big financial groups. Everything was quoted on a kind of invisible stock exchange, and the dead were worth more than the living. Sidonie moved with ease through this parallel universe. Together, we formed a great team, we were the flip sides of an era.

'Who'll be over in New York?'

'At MoMA, everyone. And the usual artists at Lowenstein and Marly.'

'Will the pigeon-roaster be there?'

'Damon Bricker will be there, yes.'

Back at home, I opted for a frozen meal endorsed by a celebrity chef whose photograph featured on the packaging. Smiling broadly beneath his tall toque, he heartily recommended the turkey breast in morel sauce, with fennel mash. I turned on the microwave and lit a pointless cigarette. What processes of the brain led me to do that, despite the lack of effect, I had no idea.

I waited for the microwave to ping. There was nothing for me to do, so I made a tour of the apartment. The Art Deco sideboard boasted a clutch of small framed photographs of Sidonie flanked by well-known artists. The same authoritative sparkle in her eye every time. I featured in just one picture. A black-and-white photograph of me with the painter Francis Bacon. He was standing with his arm around my shoulder and we were both looking at the camera, holding up glasses of champagne. Bacon was a bon viveur who liked me a lot. He was the only artist I had ever befriended. Looking at the photograph, I could hear his voice: 'Fabrice! Come and have a drink and a cigarette with me.' I told him I thought his canvases were strange and that I didn't really understand them. He reassured me, saying he felt exactly the same way about his life's work. I peered more closely at his fleshy face and slicked-back hair, always with that little lock falling artfully over his forehead. We both looked happy in the photograph. His death in Madrid in 1992 had left me genuinely saddened. Thoughts of death and mourning led me back to HBC, and I wondered what he would have thought of Franck Louvier if he had witnessed his perorations in the purple room. Is smoking allowed in the afterlife? If so, he would do as he always had when he was annoyed in life – take a long puff on his Havana cigar and pronounce the ritual words: 'That's not ideal.' Things were certainly far from ideal and I seriously doubted that Havana cigars were allowed in Paradise. But we had taken care of all that, nonetheless.

The night after HBC's death, Gold and I had spoken on the phone. We had each received a voicemail indicating that Hubert Beauchamps-Charellier's family and closest friends would be paying their last respects at his home and that we were invited. Neither Gold nor I recognised the voice of the man who had left the message, giving HBC's private address: 12 Rue Jacob, left-hand staircase, first floor, at 7 p.m. We decided to go along, but noted that Véronique Beauffancourt hadn't been invited. She had been part of HBC's immediate circle at the office, but hadn't had the same close relationship with him that we had enjoyed. At work, she said nothing, and we had studiously avoided telling her about the voicemail. If she turned up, we'd have to improvise an explanation.

We arranged to meet outside the main door of no. 12, but found one another in a cobbled courtyard, under a tree. The address was one of the finest in Saint-Germain-des-Prés: an eighteenth-century town house in which HBC owned the first-floor apartment, extending around all four sides of the courtyard. To mark the occasion, we had both decided on a black suit and matching tie – a two-tone black and navy-blue Lanvin weave for me, while Gold had found a black Versace tie with the gold head of a Medusa.

'A bit showy,' he said, 'but it's the plainest thing I've got. And Versace seemed appropriate for a case of sudden death, don't you think?'

'Queer, absolutely. Old, never,' I quipped.

'That's what I thought, too,' said Gold, perfectly seriously. 'I think he would have appreciated the gesture.'

We climbed the stone staircase and rang at the first floor. A tall, thin man with spiky white hair opened the door. He was clearly about the same age as HBC. He wore a black suit, like us, and a white shirt with a buttoned-up Mao-style collar.

'We're Jean Gold and Fabrice Valantine,' I said.

The man nodded, closing his eyes. When he opened them again, they shone with tears. He opened his mouth to speak, but nothing came. He shook us both firmly by the hand, clasping our forearms in a gesture of friendship and welcome.

'I know who you are, gentlemen,' he said finally, in a low voice.

We entered the hallway of an apartment painted entirely in black, from floor to ceiling, lit with soft lamplight. The colour was not the colour of mourning, the walls had always been like that. We followed the man along a dark corridor when he turned and spoke again.

'I'm quite forgetting myself, I'm so sorry; I'm Pierre Lachaume, Hubert's partner.' He shook both our hands once more.

The situation was tragic indeed. The poor man seemed completely lost. Gold and I exchanged a look, then continued our walk down the seemingly endless corridor. It opened onto a vast salon, also black, with its curtains drawn. About ten people were sitting on sofas and in upright armchairs. They were all men. Some were young, others not. There were no women. I wondered if HBC's family consisted only of men or whether this private adieu was a deliberately all-male gathering. I never got my answer.

The astonishingly high-ceilinged room contained dozens of small alabaster busts of men, carefully arranged, each in its own small niche, lit by an invisible spotlight. The busts were ancient Greek or Roman. This, then, was the decor of HBC's private existence: disquieting luxury, dark refinement. I had pictured him living in a huge, bright contemporary apartment. I was quite wrong. Pierre Lachaume introduced Gold and me to everyone present, describing them briefly: friend, cousin, friend, friend, art critic, journalist, antiques dealer ... Finally, we noticed an elderly – very elderly – lady, dressed all in black and seated in a black Louis XV armchair.

'Allow me to introduce Hubert's mother,' said our guide, quietly.

Gold bowed deeply from the waist and kissed her hand.

'Jean Gold. My deepest condolences. It was an honour to work with your son, Madame.'

Pierre Lachaume had positioned himself beside HBC's mother and repeated Gold's words in her ear. She nodded, with a benevolent smile.

'You are most kind, young man,' she murmured.

I followed Gold's lead and did the same.

'Fabrice Valantine. Hubert meant a great deal to me.' Suddenly, for the first time in twenty-five years, I had allowed myself to call HBC by his first name.

My comment was repeated in her ear.

'I know,' said the old lady. 'You were his appointed heir.'

Gold shot me an inquisitive look. I never gave him an explanation of her words, which I'm sure he took as the eccentricity of a near-centenarian suffering the shock of sudden bereavement. And yet, this tiny woman, bowed by age and grief, had spoken the truth. I had been Hubert's heir. An heir without a kingdom. She took my hand in hers and patted it for a few moments. I tried to catch her eye, but she stared at the wall behind me. She was blind.

'If you would like to pay your final respects, please go ahead, gentlemen,' said Pierre Lachaume. He indicated a lacquered black door standing ajar nearby.

Gold and I stepped into the bedroom. The curtains were drawn here, too. On either side of the bed, a pair of antique giltwood sconces bore two lighted church candles. HBC was lying on the red bedcover, dressed in a dinner suit, his hands folded. There was a touch of unreality to the scene, like the camp luxury of a fifties vampire movie. We stood one on each side of the bed. HBC's face wore a peaceful expression and I felt reassured. He seemed almost to be smiling. After a long silence, Gold and I looked across at each other.

'Know any prayers?' he asked.

'Not really. You?'

'Jewish prayers, but they're no use here, and I don't know them well enough, anyway. Better get on with what really matters then ...' He produced two Montecristo No. 1s from his pocket.

'What are you doing?' I asked, in horror.

'I'm respecting his last wishes.'

'What do you mean? You're mad, you're not going to smoke a cigar in here?'

'It's not for me; it's for him.'

Gold reminded me of a detail I had forgotten. How could it have escaped my mind? HBC would sometimes joke about his own death. At such moments, he would cite Errol Flynn, who was buried with six bottles of whisky in his casket, a present from his drinking companions. HBC was counting on us, his friends, he would say, to slip a few Montecristo No. 1s into his pockets before the lid on his own casket was nailed down. Gold had taken him at his word, with considerable aplomb. I was astounded. He didn't pause to question what he was doing for a second. He was simply respecting a dead man's last wish. I felt guilty. I ought to have had the same idea; I should have been the one to respect HBC's words. I had been unworthy.

Gold was bending over the body. He looked up at me.

'Ha!' he said, chuckling. 'The boss is loaded. Feel here!'

I moved closer and touched the pocket of HBC's dinner jacket. It was crammed with cigars. Everyone had carried out his instructions. Even the two trouser pockets contained a cigar each. Gold was forced to unbutton the jacket and slip two into the inside pocket. Perhaps, I thought, this was precisely why we had been invited to pay our last respects. Only those closest to the deceased had been summoned, to perform a ritual worthy of the preparations for an Egyptian mummy's journey into the afterlife. I had come empty-handed and the thought depressed me further still. Then I had an idea.

'Jean,' I said. 'What will he light his cigars with?'

'You're a bloody genius,' said Gold. 'No one's given him a lighter.'

I put my hand in my pocket. That day, God had taken mercy on the neglectful friend I had shown myself to be. The lighter I had with me was not a coloured plastic Bic, but a Cartier in brushed steel, fully loaded with gas. HBC could pass into the afterlife certain he would never be caught without a light. The Cartier was a group gift, presented to me at a small party organised to celebrate my twenty years with the firm, by an assistant with a keen sense of humour, who had left us a month later. She had been an inveterate fan of the biggest series on TV, especially one very popular at the time: *The X-Files*. The two heroes' supernatural adventures regularly brought them into contact with a cult character: the Cigarette Smoking Man. A secret service super-agent, he knew every State conspiracy, smoked incessantly and carried a lighter engraved with an iconic motto. My marvellous colleagues had arranged for it to be engraved on my gift. I slipped the lighter into HBC's breast pocket, over his now still heart. Gold recognised it and patted me on the shoulder.

'Best place for it,' he said.

The magnificent lighter was engraved with the legendary words: 'TRUST NO ONE'.

The microwave pinged. My turkey breast in morel sauce brought me back to reality. I ate my bachelor dinner at the coffee table in the sitting room, in front of the plasma TV. A glass from a bottle of Beaujolais Nouveau, reverently preserved in the fridge for the last few months, was a fitting accompaniment. I switched on the TV and selected channels at random. Jacques Dutronc was answering an interviewer's questions in his property in Corsica. Stroking a grey cat and puffing on a cigar, he proffered laconic responses whose irony seemed utterly wasted on the journalist.

'I don't know, you'd better ask him ...' he said, removing his tie mic and holding it close to his cat.

I didn't wait to hear the singer's cat's reply. I zapped.

'You claim to be in contact with François Mitterrand?' The presenter was addressing a young woman.

'Absolutely,' she replied. 'François Mitterrand's vibrations are very strong in the place where I live and we regularly hold long conversations.'

Half the studio guests were laughing openly at this. But one reminded everyone of the closing words of the late President's final New Year address to the people of France: 'I believe in the power of the spirit, and I will never leave you.' The phrase seemed to give everyone sudden pause for thought. It certainly put the wind in the spirit medium's sails.

'I've contacted Jim Morrison, too,' she persisted.

'And how's he doing?' asked the presenter.

'You shouldn't mock. I have revelations concerning his death,' she said, primly.

The turkey breast was tasty and I had all but finished the bottle of Beaujolais. All I needed was a cigarette to conclude my solitary feast. I checked my pack and saw that I had only one left. Immediately, the realisation sparked that deep dread that smokers everywhere know so well: only one cigarette left and the evening far from over. I cursed Marco Di Caro with a violence that surprised even me. For a few seconds, I genuinely wished he could be subjected to medieval-style interrogations and forced to confess to his illicit financial transactions. I pictured him bound hand and foot to a Chair of Torture, with a funnel stuffed down his throat, into which hooded henchmen poured barrels of water. I would have to go out into the night and hope to catch the tobacconist before closing time. I had done it a thousand times: trudging kilo-metres in the dark to find a *tabac* with its red sign still lit up. Each time, I had set out knowing my reward: the fond caress of the good fairy Nicotine on my body, inhalation, deliverance, pleasure. Now, the sole purpose of my quest would be to ensure there was more than one cigarette left in the entire apartment. There would be no reward, no pleasure. And what was 'pleasure' anyway? I got to my feet, opened the bookcase and took out the dictionary.

PLEASURE: noun. (From Latin *placere*, to please).
1 a. The condition or sensation induced by the experience or anticipation of what is felt to be good or desirable; a feeling of happy satisfaction or enjoyment; delight, grati-fication. Opposed to *pain*. – *I read the novel with great pleasure*. 1 b. The indulgence of physical, esp. sexual,

desires, urges or appetites; sensual or sexual gratification. to take one's pleasure: to have sexual intercourse. – *The touch of his fingers gave her such pleasure*. Pleasure principle *(psych.)*: the instinctive drive to seek pleasure and avoid pain, expressed by the id as a basic motivating force which reduces psychic tension. 1 c. Sensuous enjoyment regarded as a chief object of life or end in itself; pure enjoyment or entertainment, hedonism. Frequently contrasted with *business*. – *Are you travelling for business or pleasure?*

2. With a possessive: that which is agreeable to or in conformity with the wish or will of the person specified; will, desire, choice. – *At His (or Her) Majesty's pleasure* (of being detained in a British prison). 3. A source or object of pleasure or delight; a pleasurable experience. *It was an absolute pleasure.*

The words 'urge', 'enjoyment', 'reduces psychic tension', 'gratification', 'satisfaction' danced before my eyes. All applied perfectly to the pleasure of smoking. Alone on the sofa, I drew up a list of activities that would become devoid of meaning if their 'pleasure principle' was removed. A list like the list of cravings in the hypnotist's waiting room. The pleasure of drinking good wine, the pleasure of making love, the pleasure of smoking, of course, but also the pleasure of swimming in a lovely outdoor pool in the hot sun, the pleasure of a good meal in a good restaurant, the pleasure of a beautiful landscape, the pleasure of loving, quite simply. The pleasure of loving my cigarettes had been taken from me.

I lit my last remaining cigarette before heading out into the night in search of a fresh pack, like a great predator roaming the sleeping savannah in search of prey. The gestures. All that was left to me were the smoker's gestures, the basic motions, a reassuring presence. Clicking a lighter, lighting the cigarette, holding it between middle and index fingers, bringing it to my lips. Up until that point, all was well. After that, everything fell apart. The smoke went in and out of my lungs and then, nothing. I decided to put the cigarette out after a few puffs. If I could find no *tabac* open, I would still have that one, at least. I stubbed it out carefully on the edge of my plate. And then put the barely consumed cigarette back inside its packet, like some precious relic, and slipped it into the pocket of my navy raincoat. The weather looked stormy; a nocturnal rain shower was quite possible.

That one cigarette represented a crucial turning point in my existence: I started as an innocent man, but I would finish it a murderer.

'*Et voilà …*'

I had pronounced the words with a smile of spurious satisfaction: the *tabac* on the corner had already closed and I was alone on the pavement in the middle of the night. I must have missed the closing of the shutter by less than a minute, and that annoyed me further still. I looked to left and right. Over the years the neighbourhood had become increasingly deserted in the evenings. The store on the corner was the only shop still open. And as luck would have it, I lived near the only grocer's in Paris that did not sell cigarettes under the counter. At first, I thought this was because the owner didn't know me well enough, or distrusted me, taking me for an official inspector. But no. Months went by, then years, and I understood that, quite simply, he had no desire to sell cigarettes. What could I do? There was another grocer's much further away, on the border with the neighbouring *arrondissement*. He definitely sold cigarettes, but they wouldn't be my brand – a packet of Marlboro Light at best. The smoker is a capricious creature. When he has taken the trouble to come out at night onto the street, with a handful of *tabacs* still open, there can be no question of returning home with a packet other than his own preferred brand. The Publicis Drugstore stayed open until 2 a.m. They would have my king-size Benson & Hedges Gold. On foot it was quite a trek, but I couldn't face the thought of fetching the car from the garage beneath our building. The metro seemed the best solution. I still kept a few unused tickets in my wallet in case I ever needed them. We were four stops from the Champs-Élysées. The return journey would be quick.

I headed for the station, searching my pocket for my near-empty packet. Eventually, I gave up on the idea. I would smoke this one on my return. It would be a kind of small ritual, I told myself: when I relit it, it would signify that I had bought some more. 'And all this when it has no effect at all,' I thought, placing the pack back in my pocket.

'Scuse me! Hey! Scuse me …'

'*Et voilà* …' I said quietly, under my breath.

'Scuse me …!' The hunting cry of the predatory smoker, like a bird opening its beak in a tree-top to emit a series of harsh calls. The white-tailed eagle is a particularly good example of the latter, I seem to recall. All you can do is continue on your way without turning, pretending to be deep in thought, while imperceptibly hastening your step. At best, the predator will give up. More often, a volley of sexual insults will be directed at you or your family from behind your back.

'Scuse me … Scuse me!'

This one was following me.

There is a sub-species, the 'scuse-me-*Monsieur*' far less offensive, most probably a *lycée* student who suddenly forgets the allowance his parents pay him and takes to cadging cigarettes off strangers in the street. I would look at them and think that, perhaps, they had more money than I ever did at their age. But then cigarettes were so much cheaper in my day …

I slowed and turned, frowning. My personal 'Scuse-me' was a young man with a shaved head, dressed in military fatigues. He was small in stature and wore a hoop in one ear. He may not have been all that young, it was difficult to tell.

'Got a cigarette, mate?' he asked, as he approached.

'I haven't, sorry,' I said.

He jerked his chin in the direction of my raincoat pocket.

'You just put a pack back in there,' he said, staring me straight in the eye.

I looked back at him. What could I tell him? That the pack contained one half-smoked cigarette which I was keeping for obscure reasons of my own, which were no concern of his; that I couldn't give it to him because I had already started smoking it? I was exhausted by the whole business. And why should I have to justify myself to a stranger from out of nowhere who felt entitled to call me mate? 'Enough,' I thought. I thought it so hard that I spoke the word aloud.

'Enough,' I said and turned to walk away.

'Scuse me, scuse me! Hey!' he began again.

I dived hastily down the steps to the metro. After passing through the turnstile, I hurried along a series of tunnels, glancing back to make sure he hadn't followed me, then went down to the deserted platform. If I remembered correctly, my exit at Charles-de-Gaulle was near the rear of the train, so I headed for the far end of the platform. Once there, I shot a wary glance in the direction of the stairs. No one. He must have given up. I had already forgotten his intrusion into my evening, when I heard him yell: 'Give me a cigarette!'

He had come down the steps and was walking straight towards me. I can see him now, marching with intent. I can still feel the adrenaline rushing into my veins. The palpable tension felt by a man confronting danger. Our animal instinct returns and alarm signals are activated: predator, danger, on guard. He stopped right in front of me, in a state of high excitement, glaring defiantly.

'Give me a cigarette,' he said, as if his vocabulary was limited to a few stock phrases to be repeated over and over again.

'I don't have any I can give you,' I said, as clearly as possible, trying to maintain my calm.

'You've got a pack in your pocket,' he said.

'It's empty,' I said.

'Show me!' he ordered.

I didn't move. He glared at me and seemed drunk on his own arrogance, with his small close-set eyes and low brow. How could I have got into such an absurd situation over a mere cigarette? And how could I get out of it now? Far off, down the tunnel, I heard the mechanical rumble of the approaching metro. In a few moments I would be saved: the train would be here and my tormentor wouldn't dare follow me on board.

'Come on now, leave me alone,' I said, in deliberately weary tones. I made a show of turning away.

What followed took three seconds. I felt him grip the belt of my navy raincoat. The sensation of constraint was enough: my fear levels rocketed in the blink of an eye. I turned to face him. I saw the blade of a flick knife in his right hand. I saw the blade move towards me. I grasped his knife arm firmly at the wrist with both hands, stared him straight in the eye and toppled him onto the tracks, knife and all. The train burst out of the tunnel. There was just time to see a shape disappear beneath the driver's cabin. The brakes gave a piercing screech, loud enough to burst the eardrums of anyone within a twenty-kilometre radius. For a second, time stood still and I relived the scene in a series of flashbacks. No doubt about it, this had really happened; I had just thrown a man under a metro train. It was irreversible. 'I have to get away,' I thought. 'Get away from this platform as fast as possible. Run! Now!' I began to race towards the exit, powered by some unknown fuel. I felt as if my blood was gorged with sugar, burning calories fast. The empty tunnels raced by, with their sparkling glazed brick tiles – a thousand times more than usual, it seemed, like a vast, heavenly sky. The stairs seemed to go on for ever, too, until at last I found myself out on the street, in torrential rain. The yellow glow of the street lamps was reflected in each drop that splashed in the puddles. I was breathless. Everything was dark, the sky seemed lower and the city, smaller. I ran another fifty metres and took refuge under the eaves of a newspaper kiosk. I was shaking like a leaf. Automatically, my hands reached into my pockets for the packet of cigarettes and the lighter. Flint, spark, flame, the glow at the tip. I slid down the kiosk wall, squatted on my heels and took a long drag.

The rush; the feeling of blood accelerating in your veins; the caress of the good fairy Nicotine.

Thunder split the sky and a flash of blue lit the entire street.

The pleasure had returned.

I sat on the sofa, still in my raincoat. I had soaked the silk cushions and left pools of water on the parquet floor. Wildly, I ran through the sequence of events in my mind. I had done it because I had been afraid; I had acted in self-defence. Where would I be now if I had done nothing? In the casualty department, hovering between life and death – at best. And more likely dead. Dead in a pool of blood on the metro platform. I would have stained my nice new raincoat; no one would have come fast enough to help me. The duty station manager would have panicked before calling for an ambulance, which would have arrived too late in any event. God knows what police department would have called Sidonie on her mobile in New York, then contacted Emma in Barcelona. A tragedy. I had avoided that, at least, but – and this was perhaps the most difficult part to acknowledge – fear, panic and the survival instinct weren't all I had felt in those three fateful seconds. My attacker's murderous impulse had sparked the same in me. I had hurled him onto the metro tracks quite deliberately. The gesture was an expression of irrational rage, an overpowering need for immediate retaliation – a lightning reaction that he had completely failed to anticipate. No fifty-year-old in a navy raincoat would put up a fight. And he was right, I hadn't put up a fight; I had killed him outright. I thought of the dictionary definition: 'a feeling of happy satisfaction or enjoyment; delight, gratification. Opposed to *pain*.' The definition of 'pleasure'. I had acted with a degree of pleasure. The hardest thing of all to admit. He had wanted to torment me, stick a knife in me, put an end to my life. As if I didn't have enough worries at the moment. He had paid for all the rest; he had seen what happened to anyone who attempted to cross Fabrice Valantine.

Pleasure in the act of killing: that was what I had felt; that was the appalling truth. That pleasure had brought back the enjoyment of smoking, like an added bonus, a reward. The ultimate transgression had smashed all the barriers in my brain, set my personal history back to zero. At twenty minutes past midnight precisely, I had crossed to the other side, and now belonged to that select band of those who have committed murder.

I got to my feet, feeling a sudden urge to be sick. I emerged from the toilet feeling groggy, having emptied my stomach of the Beaujolais and the turkey breast in morel sauce. I removed my navy raincoat, my jacket, my white shirt, and stood there, bare-chested, in the middle of the sitting room, like some great disorientated mammal, before heading to the bathroom to splash water on my face and rinse my mouth with Eau de Botot. Back in the sitting room, I stepped out onto the balcony, to see an ambulance and a police van in the street below. Their roof lights rotated in silence in front of the entrance to the metro. I was the person responsible for all of this. I fetched my mobile to take a picture – a way of convincing myself that this was really happening, that it wasn't a dream. On my small screen, the blue and red lights were all that could be seen against a dark background. An abstract work of sorts. I pressed the button to immortalise the moment. I was the only person who would know the meaning of this blurred photograph.

The next day, after two telephone calls from my womenfolk, letting me know they had arrived safely, I went to buy a packet of cigarettes from the kiosk. I had taken barely a puff before I was forced to acknowledge that the euphoria produced by the previous night's events had vanished. Once again, the smoke tasted of nothing but dust. My alpha and beta molecules had sunk back into their coma. The pleasure had returned only in the immediate aftermath of the crime. Would I be forced to commit serial homicides in order to enjoy a cigarette? No. It had not come to that yet.

And what about guilt? I hear you ask. With hindsight, my personal experience has taught me a few things. I would say that any criminal who feels excessively high levels of guilt is likely to quit after his first outing and won't make a career of it. You need to detach yourself as quickly as possible from the many heightened emotions provoked by committing a crime, rather like a lottery winner who becomes a millionaire, but carries on working and changes nothing at all about their way of life. Such people are wise indeed. It takes a certain wisdom to successfully carry out a crime – a premeditated crime, I mean, which was not the case with my first one. But my actions had afforded me an insight into my own relatively limited capacity for remorse. Doubtless some criminals would ponder and fret until they drove themselves to madness or suicide, but I was not of their number. In truth, the crime had whipped me smartly back into shape at a time when I had all but succumbed to the siren song of melancholy.

And so I began my first day as a 'criminal'. The invisible taint, known only to myself, would be with me for the rest of my life. Living with a secret can be a burden, but it can be exciting too. I had discovered a new power, a vast power I had been completely unaware of until now. Everyone carries this Pandora's box around with them, deeply concealed. Some have opened it just a crack and snapped it shut again immediately. Others make use of it. Serial killers – a category that sprang rapidly to mind – exploited its darkest side. The military, too. The strategies of war which bring about the great geopolitical upheavals of the world are ultimately based on nothing but murder on a grand scale as a powerful means of persuasion. Such a grand scale at times, that the crimes committed become abstract. The genocide of tens of thousands of people on the other side of the world is less real to us than a random news item involving a jealous partner and a .22 long rifle. The ability to make death abstract is a trick valued highly by the dictators of this world. Grand illusionists that they are, they can make entire populations disappear without anyone worrying about it. A rabbit, a hat, and abracadabra, no more rabbit. It will be years before the audience discovers that the empty hat is soaked in blood. Light years from these criminal masterminds, murderers like me are mere artisans, plying our lowly trade. But sometimes, like every gifted craftsman, we come close to attaining Art with a capital A.

Like any self-respecting criminal, I returned to the scene of my crime. Before fetching my car from the garage beneath our building, I went down into the metro, not without a certain feeling of apprehension. I had the strange impression that everyone could read my mind. That if I looked someone in the eye, they would freeze and speak to me: 'Wasn't it you who hurled your attacker under the train last night?' I threaded my way through the crowd to the platform's end. Nothing. There was no trace of the events of the night before. The tracks were spotless and the daytime hubbub made the station feel so different that it seemed as if my crime had been committed very long ago, in another dimension. It was true, I would venture to say in my defence, that this murder had been a rather special case. I hadn't pursued an innocent victim in order to take their life in some hideous way; no, the young man I had tossed onto the tracks was no lamb, and his knife had already been used once that evening. I gleaned that over lunch from the 'News in Brief' section of *Le Parisien*.

With the departure of the beautiful but tobacco-hating blonde, we had deserted the canteen at HBC Consulting once more and returned to our haunts in nearby cafés. That lunchtime, I ate at the Bon Coin with Gold and Véronique. Jean Verider, quiet and withdrawn for the past few days, was eating nearby at the counter. Delighted to have us back, the café owner had offered us all a *kir* before our meal. Véronique had asked for a copy of *Le Parisien* and began poring over its pages.

'Good riddance,' she muttered, as the waiter brought our calves' liver in raspberry vinegar.

Gold leaned over the paper.

'What's that?' I asked.

'Some guy was thrown under a train, right opposite your place. You should keep up with the news in your own neighbourhood!' joked Gold, tucking his napkin into his shirt collar.

'Around half past midnight,' added Véronique.

'I was asleep,' I said. 'What does it say?'

'"The man, in his early thirties, was pushed onto the tracks by an unknown passenger,"' read Véronique, "'on the night of Tuesday to Wednesday and died instantly. The police are investigating the possibility of gang violence or a mugging. The man, as yet unidentified, had attacked a young woman earlier in the evening in a private car park on the Plaine Monceau. The woman is being treated in hospital for a knife wound. Her jewellery was found in the man's pockets."

'Well, good riddance, I say!' she said again. 'He tried attacking someone else and she fought back.'

'Or he,' I said, chewing my calves' liver.

'Can you imagine,' said Gold, 'throwing someone under a train.'

'No, I can't,' I said.

'You're home alone at the moment,' he went on. 'How about dinner?'

He turned to Véronique.

'Véronique, what do you say to dinner with a couple of old bachelors, one of whom is married?'

'An offer I can't refuse ...' she said, coyly.

Gold's campaign of seduction, rolled out over the past few weeks, was bearing fruit.

'No need to get together over dinner,' growled Jean Verider from the bar, where he was finishing a glass of beer. 'We're all going to be seeing one another after work sooner than you know, and we'll be practically stark naked, too!'

We stared at one another in silence.

'Jean, have you been drinking?' Véronique asked him, quietly.

'Haven't you checked your email? The boss dropped his little surprise just before lunch.'

'He's taking us all to a swingers' club?' speculated Gold.

'If only,' grumbled Verider. 'It's worse than that. We're off to a pool party.'

Verider was right. My inbox contained two unopened messages. The first was from Franck Faye, letting me know that things were going wonderfully well at Kerko Beijing. He had attached a photograph of himself in a pilot's jumpsuit, standing in front of a model aeroplane. He held the remote control in both hands with the antenna pointed towards the lens. The words 'Cleared for take-off!' were inscribed in large purple letters in the sky above. I wrote back: 'This is ATC Valantine wishing you an enjoyable flight – over and out!'

The second message was internal. Subject line: *In at the deep end!*

HBC Consulting / Internal mail / 12:57
We're all in this together! So let's break the ice and pool our synergies for even greater success going forward. This Friday, HBC Consulting takes the plunge at the Piscine Pontoise, in the fifth arrondissement. This iconic gem of thirties architecture will open exclusively for all department heads, research assistants and staff. Join us for a fun, friendly evening swim from 6 p.m. to midnight: coach transport from outside the building. Bring your swimming things, and come on in!
Franck Louvier
CEO, HBC Consulting

I hurried to search for more information about the pool in question. There were several online reviews:

My favourite Paris pool! Magnificent architecture, great size (thirty-three metres!), better opening hours than most of the city's other municipal pools. I love the late-night openings, with special underwater lighting and background music, perfect for a relaxing swim after work. Warm water, and hot, clean showers. Powerful hairdryers, and there's a small space with a mirror and shelf so you can do your hair and make-up before leaving. The only downside is the price, which is slightly higher than other pools: admission has been increased for the evening sessions to around nine euros, I think (?), which is really a bit much, but it does include access to the gym and sauna. But the pool is the only thing I'm interested in, so … Great changing rooms, too, with balconies overlooking the pool, but sometimes you have to wait up to five minutes for a member of staff to open your cubicle. Apart from that, the people are polite and friendly, especially the ticket-sellers. Long queues in summer, try to avoid peak times.

Pontoise would be perfect if the pool was a full fifty metres. Completely different atmosphere to other municipal pools, the staff are friendly, smiling, helpful. As well as the pool, there's a gym, a sauna, etc. But you have to pay extra for that (about twenty euros for a full day). Anyway, back to the pool: when you arrive, take the stairs up to the changing rooms. There's a space where everyone leaves their shoes. The cubicles are arranged over two levels. An attendant will show you where you can leave your stuff, and unlock the cubicle when you come back. The floor's clean and the cubicles are spacious. After changing, you go back downstairs to the showers, which have all the charm of a prison washroom (not that I've ever been to prison, haha, but you get the picture); anyway the plumbing is a bit outdated, but it's all clean and well-maintained (apart from an old, rusty radiator in the men's showers). Ditto the toilets — never seen such clean toilets in a public swimming pool before. And then finally, you reach the pool which is thirty-three metres long, so not bad for a decent swim really. One metre deep at one end, two metres sixty at the other, with five lanes. The water's very clear and clean, with modern tiles. Swimmers are generally well-behaved. A great place for a relaxing swim. I went on a Monday afternoon. They have late-night opening some evenings, until midnight. But then it costs ten euros ... But you get access to all the other stuff I mentioned above (sauna, gym, fitness classes, etc.) and there's music (according to the lifeguard I spoke to). Must try it sometime!

I was a broken man. Obviously, any refusal to go along would be very poorly viewed. Franck Louvier had cornered us all like rats in a maze with his grotesque invitation and his chlorine-drenched synergy-pooling. I was darkly pondering the prospect when my telephone rang.

'I've looked it up online,' said Véronique, getting straight to the point.

'Me too,' I said. 'Apparently, they have underwater lighting in the evenings ...'

'I'm not bothered about the pool!' said Véronique. 'I am *not* appearing in front of the entire office in my swimming costume.'

'You know you'll have to, Véronique,' I said wearily. 'And anyway, you'll look very pretty and Jean will be delighted.'

She stammered a few words of annoyance and hung up. This swimming soirée was to surpass even my worst fears.

The pool was lit from below the waterline. Through the great glass ceiling overhead, you could see night falling to the gentle rhythms of the elevator muzak that echoed through the huge building. I had shut the door of my second-floor cubicle behind me and was preparing to make my way down to the pool in my red swimming trunks, towel over one shoulder and a grey swimming cap on my head. A quick glance in the mirror heightened my feelings of irritation: I looked ridiculous in the vile cap that clung to me like a second scalp. As if I'd gone suddenly bald and decided to spray my head silver.

'Ludicrous,' I muttered, and began walking along the cubicles.

One of them opened and Véronique appeared in a black one-piece bathing suit and a white cap.

'Just look at me! Cellulite! All you can see is my cellulite!' she wailed.

'Absolutely not,' I said.

'Absolutely yes!'

Gold waved from the other side, then made his way over towards us.

'Thought I'd wear my Hawaiian bermudas!' He winked.

We stared at his brightly coloured shorts, printed with a pattern of small sharks attempting to sink their teeth into hapless surfers. Around his neck, he wore a fine gold chain with a Star of David and a grey baroque pearl.

'You look superb,' he told Véronique.

'No I don't …' she sighed.

'But you do,' Gold persisted.

'No, I do not!' retorted Véronique.

They continued in this vein as we made our way down to the first floor. From the balcony, we looked down on a handful of research assistants venturing cautiously into the water. They waved cheerfully. I decided we looked like a herd of animals that had reached a waterhole and stood hesitating on the brink, before getting wet. Sabine, our departmental secretary, touched the surface with an outstretched toe, like a prima ballerina.

'Sabine's got a fantastic figure,' said Gold, spontaneously.

A flash of terror shot through Véronique's eyes.

'Well, now's your chance! What are you waiting for?' she said, rather too sharply.

Gold shrugged his shoulders. Véronique's wrath was wasted on him. He reminded us that Sabine was twenty-seven, he was old enough to be her father, and would look a fine fool if he tried. He concluded that, in any case, Sabine was blonde and he didn't like blondes; they reminded him of his first wife, and that was a bad memory. I stared at my own practically hairless chest, then my stomach, and pulled it in a little with a discreet clenching of the muscles. It was quite easy to keep it up and would make me look a little slimmer. I then glanced at Gold's stomach and thought to myself that he should do the same.

'You're hairy,' I told him.

'Yes. Always have been,' he replied.

'Not as a child, surely?'

'No, not as a child,' he agreed.

Our personal observations brought us to the foot bath, through which we had to pass before reaching the showers. Gold leaned across and whispered something in Véronique's ear. Her smile returned; the reference to Sabine was forgotten. In the showers, I looked around for the old, rusty radiator mentioned by the Internet reviewer, but was unable to spot it. The sight of the entire office staff in swimsuits was certainly strange. Bizarrely immodest. Some people looked taller or smaller than usual. The women had bigger or smaller chests than one might have thought. I wondered what my colleagues thought about me. They, too, would be thinking: 'Goodness, Valentine isn't hairy at all, and he's musclier than I thought.' Or perhaps the reverse.

Jean Verider marched through the showers, greeting no one. We caught a brief glimpse of a white extra-large T-shirt printed with a naked girl in a Playboy pose, the height of vulgarity. Exiting the showers, we found him pacing around the edge of the pool. He looked huge in his T-shirt and shorter than usual, too. When fully dressed, he almost certainly wore compensatory soles in the heels of his loafers. He had tiny feet, too, like a child's. His stick-thin legs supported an outsize trunk and a stomach it was pointless to try and hold in. The T-shirt bore the legend 'Life's a bitch' in sky-blue letters above the naked blonde who was kneeling suggestively on all fours, her eyes rolling back, tongue lolling half out of her mouth.

'If I'm told to dress for the beach, I dress for the beach!' he told us all, before anyone could say a word.

'Jean, that's a bit excessive,' said Véronique.

He nodded nervously and went to sit in a white plastic chair, like a lifeguard surveying us all. We stepped slowly into the water, pausing to shake the hands of a few colleagues splashing about in front of a pressure jet nearby. Shaking hands underwater is something you have to try in order to appreciate the full absurdity of the gesture.

'Good evening, everyone! Welcome!'

We jumped out of our skins. Franck Louvier's voice resonated from every loudspeaker around the pool. He was standing on the diving board, microphone in hand. His athletic musculature gleamed, but not with pool water: he must have slathered himself in oil, like a bodybuilder. He delivered a short speech about the Piscine Pontoise, a gem of thirties architecture, with its thirty-three-metre pool, and about how we would all get to know one another better through the joy of sport, and other nonsense. He looked like an Aryan SS officer, glamorised in a film by Leni Riefenstahl. With his short blond slightly swept-back hair, a black-and-white photograph of him would easily pass for an old piece of Nazi propaganda.

'I'd just like to remind you that all the pool's facilities are yours for the evening: the sauna, hammam, squash court and gym. Thank you, everyone, and enjoy your evening! I'm coming over to see you, Monsieur Verider,' he concluded, before handing his mic to one of his yes-men.

Our new leader flexed his muscles, left his perch in a perfect dive and raced through the water like a torpedo towards Jean Verider, who had risen to his feet and stood watching the approach of his boss, part man, part fish. A brief, lively exchange ensued. We caught the words 'obscene' and 'disgraceful', after which the fish-man slid back into the water while Verider removed his T-shirt, screwed it into a ball and threw it angrily to the floor next to his chair.

'I'll go and talk to him,' said Véronique, moving off to join her colleague in a few graceful strokes.

'Sabine! I didn't know you had a tattoo,' exclaimed Gold.

The young woman was swimming beside us and blushed deeply. She turned to allow us to admire the motif on her back, a sort of yellow and red butterfly, vaguely Japanese in style, a birthday present from her boyfriend.

'It's meant to bring good luck in love!' she told us with a

radiant smile before kicking her legs and disappearing with a splash.

At the other end of the pool, Véronique was talking to Jean Verider. She had convinced him to get into the water. Around us, the younger staff had challenged Franck Louvier to a race. The man was a machine, executing a perfect, relentless butterfly, his shoulders ploughing mechanically through the water. With their summer-holiday front crawl, the others had a job to keep up.

'He's the fucking Terminator,' said Gold.

Véronique drew level with us, followed by Verider, who splashed along, glaring furiously all around him. He looked like a partly submerged owl. His pectorals were enhanced by two little rolls of fat, a phenomenon I had noticed at the beach in other overweight men: they often developed something akin to the breasts of a young girl. The effect was especially horrible here. Verider glowered at Franck Louvier, who was still ploughing up and down the pool. Finally, Louvier sprang nimbly from the water and stood at the edge of the pool, where he performed a few stretches before flipping onto his stomach like a carp and beginning a series of press-ups. He clapped his hands together between each one and repeated the entire sequence over again. He was inexhaustible.

Verider watched him, stony-faced. I knew that look. I had seen it once, for a fraction of a second, on a metro platform. The expression was that of a man in the grip of a murderous impulse. Verider was experiencing it now, for sure, just as I had then. Though accomplishing the act would be somewhat harder in the middle of a busy swimming pool.

'If only he could die of a heart attack like HBC ...' he said, feelingly.

I made no reply. None was expected. He had muttered the

words to himself before heading for the stairs, saying nothing more to anyone. I turned and looked around for Gold and Véronique. They had got out of the water. Gold was talking to her and showing her his baroque pearl.

'Fabrice!'

Louvier was calling me. He slipped back into the pool. With three powerful strokes he was at my side.

'Listen, Fabrice – I plan to reorganise the first floor completely. I'm going to move you down to the basement.'

It took a few seconds for the words to sink in.

'Did you hear what I said? Have you got water in your ears?' he laughed.

'You want to send me back down to the basement?'

'"Send you back down"? It's not like that ... You'll have a bigger office. It'll be a windowless space, but we'll install daylight lamps. It'll look terrific,' he concluded, with a broad smile.

It was at that moment I decided to kill him.

The planning of a crime is exciting for the criminal. Everything has to be thought through and carefully organised. Probabilities, unforeseen circumstances and exact timings are the elements that must all be considered and a touch of genius added. The cocktail is best mixed when you're feeling on top form. It's a little like planning for a trip, but more finely tuned. And you won't be the person taking the one-way ticket. Suicides excepted, of course. The latter always appear to brighten up shortly before carrying out their plan, so it seems, leaving their nearest and dearest more bewildered still. There's a very simple explanation for this: they are motivated by the murder they're about to commit.

The urge to kill can be a powerful driver in life, and carrying out the perfect murder is very rewarding. For me, the reward was heightened by an additional pleasure: an intoxicating cigarette, the nicotine coursing through my veins, my head spinning and a delicious frisson in my lungs. When I next experienced the joy of smoking, Franck Louvier would be entering the afterlife. The first time, I had hurled a man who wanted to kill me under a metro train. The context was subtler this time, but the motive was the same: I was defending my own self-interest. I was the hunter, always. Never the prey.

How to kill? There are thousands of ways to kill your neighbour, but few will pass unnoticed. Getting hold of a revolver is difficult in France; guns make a great deal of noise and do a fair amount of damage. And ballistics experts can trace a weapon by the bullets it fires, following the trail back to you. A knife demands a strong nerve and a level of dexterity I did not possess.

A stroll through the Internet led me to blogs I could never have imagined existed. I began by entering various phrases into my search engine: 'how to kill your boss', 'how to get rid of an enemy', 'how to make someone disappear', but eventually settled on a few internationally recognised keywords like 'kill', 'murder' and 'crime'. The words were contained in an extraordinary range of blogs, mostly focused on films or music, until at length I came upon an American website.

At first glance, there was nothing sinister in the photograph of a respectable elderly man surrounded by a cluster of grandchildren; still less so in the blog's title: 'Grandpa Edward's Good Ol' Stories'. The CIA logo in the top right-hand corner of the homepage was intriguing, and a click on a photograph of Grandpa Edward as a young American army officer led to his biography. Was the old man telling his round-eyed little ones his wartime memories? Yes, he was. But these were not the usual old soldier's tales, brimming with nostalgia and patriotism. Far from it.

Old Grandpa Edward had been enlisted in the American intelligence services for the Normandy landings. He had entered the dark world of secret and special agents and never left. The termination with extreme prejudice of the many enemies of the United States had become his personal speciality. 'Know this, my darling young ones: your grandpa, or your great-grandpa for the littlest ones among you, who is now growing very, very old, committed no fewer than fifty-seven homicides for the noble cause of American democracy. I'm going to tell all you little critters in the land of childhood how your old, loving grandpa eliminated all the bad guys who tried to bring down the great country of Abraham Lincoln.'

Photographs of this kindly old grandfather, children on his knee and a book open in one hand, punctuated tales that had more to do with strangulation techniques and punctured carotid arteries than with Goldilocks and apple pie. The site was a criminal's Bible. As far as I could make out, the patriarch welcomed his entire family once a month, when he would tell them – for digital posterity – the story of another killing, to be related on the family blog that had been set up by his loved ones two years previously. The result was an appalling combination of 'memoirs of a serial killer' and a brochure advertising round-the-world plane tickets: 'How I Killed in Vietnam', 'How I Killed in South America', 'How I Killed in Russia' and so on. Each experience was described in abundant detail; sometimes, the narrative was illustrated with diagrams drawn by the old man's trembling hand. Perhaps one of these methods could be adapted for Franck Louvier? But Grandpa Edward's crimes were so extraordinary that reproducing them outside their original military context would not be easy.

'My old chum John Minnery,' I read under a photograph of Edward and another man, taken several decades ago.

'John is the author of a marvellous book, aptly titled *How to Kill: The Complete Guide to Killing without Pleasure*,' the blog continued. I immediately opened another tab on my screen and began searching for the book. It had never been translated into French and was currently unavailable. I went back to Grandpa Edward's page. There was a knock at my office door. One of Franck Louvier's minions, a thirty-year-old in a grey three-piece suit and, of course, no tie, asked me if I was free to take a look at the lower-ground-floor space with him.

'Not just now,' I answered drily. 'I'm busy with a project for Monsieur Louvier, as it happens.'

He didn't press the point and closed the door behind him with elaborate care. Grandpa Edward's criminal adventures were instructive, but provided few firm leads. I reclined in my black leather office chair and tipped it slowly back and forth, thinking, when Jean Verider's words came to mind: 'If only he could die of a heart attack like HBC ...' There was my answer. Old Grandpa Edward had described one or two poisonings among his murders, but I had discounted that possibility: he made use of substances it was almost impossible to come by, like cyanide and dioxin. My own method would be simpler, but every bit as effective; it required a weapon only a dedicated herpetologist would think of, a weapon capable of killing ten men at a stroke, a weapon measuring three centimetres in length, found only in the rainforests of South America: *Phyllobates terribilis*. One touch of the golden poison frog's skin and the countdown would begin.

A man would die of a heart attack in Paris: who for one second would imagine that he had been in contact with a frog found only in the borderlands of Ecuador and Colombia?

Back at home, I reviewed every possible means of acquiring the fabulous frog. There was a good chance I would find one in private hands, but when golden poison frogs are bred in captivity, they lose their toxicity. I needed a wild specimen. Back at my screen, I consulted forums and blogs dedicated to herpetology. The online jungle ... The comparison was a good one. When it came to exotic animals, the Web was a teeming virtual Amazonia. With the explosion of digital photography, every frog-fancier was posting pictures of their favourite creature. Hundreds of thousands of images were circulating online. In my day, all we had were two bimonthly magazines, available on subscription, through which to exchange our news and infor-mation. On the 'Readers' Questions' page, a query as to the best source of a particular species of gecko would be answered a full two months later. Times had changed: now, you could Google the question and find your answer in seconds. I was peering at my screen, searching for frog experts, when a shout rang out in the central courtyard.

'Here we go again,' I muttered.

Our neighbours in the building included a couple who had moved in about a year before, since when it had become apparent that the husband beat his wife. They lived in another part of the block, but our apartments were reached from the same courtyard. A violent row had broken out the previous summer while I was away. Sidonie had gone over to their staircase and threatened to call the police.

'Why don't you report him?' she had shouted to the woman.

The husband had flung their door open with considerable force. Sidonie had backed away, afraid he would beat her too.

'I'm warning you, I've got connections. If you touch a hair on my head, you'll be answering to a Minister of State,' she had told him.

The incident had gone no further. Since then, we had often encountered the wife in her dark glasses; she never spoke to us, and I must confess I never dared say a word to her. This time, the sound of breaking glass startled me as I sat in my desk chair. A window pane, for sure, because I heard the shards of glass falling into the courtyard below. I went to the kitchen window, the only one in our apartment that looked onto the courtyard, apart from Emma's bedroom. I saw a lamp, still lit, overturned in the darkness of their living room, and a figure picking it up. By the light of the bulb, my eyes met those of the man: Pascal Brunet, third floor, building B, staircase C. He stared at me for a fraction of a second before tugging sharply at the lead and socket. The light was extinguished, but his face remained burned on my retina, in the clash of darkness and light. It's never a good idea for an evil bastard to imprint himself on the retina of a murderer. I don't advise it: it might lead to an idea for a spot of entertainment on an idle afternoon. He beat his wife and I was looking for ways to kill my boss. Two highly dangerous predators had just stared at one another in the night. Our paths would cross again in broad daylight.

I returned to my screen, but listened out for further noise. If I heard anything, I would call the emergency services. I heard nothing.

The online forum Herpetomania contained a formidable number of documents on reptiles and amphibians. Hundreds of pythons, dozens of chameleons. Once you had signed up and chosen a pseudonym, you could chat with other members. I became Natrix Natrix. Now authorised to answer queries and ask questions of my own, I amused myself for a while, telling beginners about the characteristics of ladder snakes or the correct food for iguanas. I used keyword searches to try and locate a *Phyllobates terribilis* enthusiast. Sure enough, I found one in the small ads section: the digital age had spelled the end of the paper editions of the magazines devoted to amateur herpetology, but this vital section remained virtually unchanged online. Majortom888 was selling the precious merchandise I sought: 'Hi everyone,' he began, 'Currently AWOL in frog-keepers' paradise: Colombia, near the Rio Patia. Frogs everywhere, and I plan to bring back a few wild specimens of *Phyllobates terribilis* (they really are fluorescent yellow when observed out here). Anyone who fancies keeping one of these little guys can contact me by email to arrange a discreet Paris meet-up (no questions asked). Ciao.'

He had posted the message that morning and would be returning to Paris the next day. Immediately, I left a reply signed with my new *nom de guerre*, Natrix Natrix. I told him I could collect a specimen as soon as he liked, and he could name his price. The wheels were in motion; everything was going perfectly. I would succeed. In my excitement, I had quite forgotten to eat and decided to smoke a cigarette instead. My impulse to murder must have been strong, because I was surprised to feel a small, very small something. The pleasure signal was blinking up ahead, through the fog, over the waters of my unconscious. The faint gleam of a lighthouse that said: 'Come.' Yes, I would come. In fact, I was well on my way.

I had bought a bouquet of roses for Sidonie's return.

'The best you have,' I told the girl in the shop.

The bill was unexpected, to say the least, but the flowers were magnificent. Sidonie had refused my offer to meet her at the airport. She would come back in a taxi, she said; it would be easier. The only possible hitch, I thought, was that her homecoming dinner would be cut short. Majortom888 had arranged a meeting at 11 p.m. in an Irish pub near Châtelet. This was the only day and time he would be in Paris; after that he was heading south. I had agreed and was wondering how I could explain to Sidonie that I would be going out immediately after dinner. The question preoccupied me all day. Eventually, I came up with a plan that might work. Gold would have some sort of crisis at around 10 p.m. and call me to see if I wanted to meet him for a drink. I had adapted the alarm on my phone, replaced it with my usual ringtone, and programmed the 'call' for 10 p.m. I would pretend to answer and have a short conversation with my colleague. Then I would say to Sidonie: 'Poor old Gold, he's been feeling low lately. I don't think he's getting anywhere with Véronique. He wants to meet for a drink, he's quite close by.' To which Sidonie would very likely reply: 'Absolutely, go and have a drink with your friend,' or words to that effect. I had worked up the details of the plan at the St James Club while waiting to meet a new candidate, one who wasn't quite right, in my opinion. It's not every day you make a match like Franck Faye and Kerko Beijing.

When Sidonie came through the front door with her two suit-cases, I could tell something was wrong.

'Is anything the matter?' I asked.

'No, why?' she answered, quickly.

'You look annoyed.'

'Not at all. I'm tired. It's a seven-hour flight now that Concorde's gone,' she grumbled.

She added that it was probably her make-up, which had worn off while she slept on the plane.

She seemed to like the bouquet of roses. She asked me the name of the florist where I had bought them, but I'd forgotten. We spoke little over dinner – I knew my wife was tired and respected that. We talked about Emma, who had sent two emails to her mother. She seemed to be having fun in Barcelona. Sidonie noted that our daughter had stopped talking about giving up smoking and she suspected, as did I, that she wasn't keeping her promise. Between mouthfuls of chicken tandoori, I examined the American press reviews of her exhibition. Photos of artists I didn't know, as usual, except for the pigeon-blaster, grinning like a film star in every shot. He might have been Tom Cruise.

'He seems like a happy soul,' I said, quietly.

Sidonie didn't reply, but cautiously held out a photograph of herself taken by a famous American photographer. He had organised a shoot with her almost a year ago, in Paris, during Photography Month, and had presented her with the print during her trip to New York.

'It's hideous,' I said.

'Not at all, it's wonderful, Fabrice.'

Joel-Peter Witkin (for that was his name) had photographed

156

my wife in profile, eyes closed, in black and white, and had then retouched the photograph with unbearable realism, transforming it into a still life. Sidonie's head looked as if it had been severed with an axe, then placed on a wooden table, surrounded by old cooking utensils and small insects that seemed to be pondering this curious dish and how best to set about devouring it. The background was radiant with light, and the whole thing was suffused with a quasi-funereal sense of calm.

'Joel-Peter's work is all about death,' Sidonie told me earnestly.

'I can see that. Will you frame it and hang it in the sitting room?'

'No. It's for my personal archive,' she said, swallowing a mouthful of burgundy.

Just at that moment, my telephone rang. I performed my little scene with aplomb.

'Go and have a drink with your friend,' suggested my wife, as I had hoped she would.

I was almost disappointed. My deceit, which even someone cheating in his wife would have failed to carry off quite so convincingly, deserved recognition. Secretly, I should have liked her to discover the truth. To frown and ask why Gold was calling so late in the evening, which was most unlike him, and to ask me if I was in fact meeting a woman. Deep down, I wanted her to feel suspicious and raise her eyebrows in surprise, though it would have disrupted all my plans. But she did nothing like that. I could set out for a made-up rendezvous late at night and she wasn't in the least bothered. 'Go and have a drink with your friend.' So be it. I would go and have a drink with Majortom888.

As I was putting on my navy raincoat, she kissed me full on the mouth. I returned the kiss, with a smile.

'Thank you for the roses,' she said, before announcing that she was tired and would be going to bed.

I set out into the night to meet my *Phyllobates terribilis*.

Eleven o'clock in the evening. The pub was quite empty, which surprised me, as the cafés I had passed on my way were all crowded with people. A long bar, dark wooden tables and walls lined with film and sporting posters in English. I looked around for Majortom888. The old man sitting at a table in the corner with his Guinness was an unlikely match for the pseudonym, as was the blonde girl next to him, staring fixedly at the bottles of whisky. I moved forward into the main room. A group of boys were laughing noisily between gulps of beer, while a handful of couples sipped their drinks and gazed into one another's eyes. At one table, a young man was sitting with his back to me, his blond hair in dreadlocks like my daughter's. His were threaded with red yarn. I moved closer until I could see his face. Twenty-five at most, pale complexion, two piercings in each eyebrow, and a small goatee beard, also blond, twisted into a point.

'Are you Majortom888?'

'That's me!' he answered, reaching out to shake my hand. 'You must be Natrix Natrix?'

I nodded and sat down opposite him. He was drinking a Guinness.

'The same,' I said to the waitress who was heading our way. She turned back to the bar immediately.

'So how was Colombia?' I asked, to open the conversation.

'It was cool. Crazy,' he replied enthusiastically. 'Y'know, we can call each other *tu*, man,' he added, keeping things informal. I ignored the suggestion. *Vous* it would be.

'So you're a herpetologist?' I asked.

'Yep. I am *really* into reptiles!' he confirmed.

I had taken him for an uninformed amateur, but I was wrong. Our conversation convinced me that behind his techno-tribal get-up and youthful, hip vocabulary (Véronique would have dismissed him as a 'roadman' in the current parlance) he was an erudite enthusiast, very well informed on a wide range of species. In my day, herpetology was a field reserved for extremely, even troublingly, serious and earnest types. Clearly, the species had mutated. After my second Guinness, I asked him outright: 'So, my *Phyllobates*, have you got it with you?'

'Sure. Listen, man, it was an expensive trip. I know you're going to think this is well out of order, but I'm gonna need a hundred and fifty euros.'

I nodded in silence. In fact, I'd been expecting far more. I had even brought a €500 note with me. The price came as a surprise, but a good one. The young man clearly didn't have the same relationship to money as I did. And he lacked a certain business acumen. In his position, seeing me arrive in my three-piece grey suit, with my designer shirt and silver cufflinks, I would have doubled my price. I removed one €100 note and one €50 note from my wallet and laid them on the table.

'Cool,' he said, picking up the money.

'And the frog?' I asked.

He gave a small conspiratorial smile and put his hand in the pocket of his denim jacket, which was stitched with a patch declaring 'Jesus forever'.

'You can go and check it out in the toilets,' he said, before slipping something under the table for me.

I felt around and my hand touched a small cylinder covered in aluminium foil.

'Are you sure it's just come from Colombia?' I asked. I felt suddenly worried. 'It wasn't bred in captivity?'

He responded with another conspiratorial smile. He searched in another pocket, stitched with a badge bearing a word in English whose meaning escaped me: 'Prodigy'. He took out a French passport, opened it at the stamped pages and held it out for me to inspect. The colourful Colombia stamp covered the whole page, and the date was correct. No doubt about it – he had just returned.

'You're right to check, man; I'm really careful when I buy shit, too.'

'I don't doubt it,' I replied.

I got up to look for the toilets.

'Another drink?' I asked.

'Yeah, same again.'

'It's on me,' I said, making a sign at the waitress.

The toilets' neon lights gave a strange yellowish glow. Next to the mirror and the dubious-looking washbasin, some jokers had scrawled an enemy's name, a brief list of his supposed sexual specialities, and a phone number. I toyed with the idea of adding Franck Louvier's, but no, I had something much better in store for him. The aluminium foil covered a glass test tube, carefully sealed with a piece of gauze and a cork plug. There was a tiny pinhole at the top for air. At the other, rounded end, Majortom888 had placed a little moist earth. And there, on a tiny piece of moss, sat *Phyllobates terribilis*. Minuscule, glossy, with near-fluorescent yellow-green skin. The frog turned its head and looked at me with its inky-black eyes. The ultimate weapon. The last time I had seen one was a long time ago, in my bedroom at home. Nothing remained from those days, but the frog had returned from the past to help me commit my first premeditated murder. I slipped the tube into my jacket pocket and left the toilets. Majortom888 was still sitting at his table, about to drink from a fresh Guinness. He turned to me.

'So?'

'We've met. Perfect.'

'Told you,' he said, tilting his glass towards mine while I seated myself back down opposite him.

'Your very good health!'

'And yours,' I said, smiling more to myself than at him.

The toast was nothing if not ironic.

Back at home, I opened the front door as quietly as possible and headed for the bedroom, where Sidonie lay sleeping in the darkness. I took the test tube from my pocket to examine it by the light of a lamp: the frog was less than three centimetres long. With the little suckers on its toes and the grain of its fluorescent-yellow skin, it made a delightful, fascinating novelty. I was counting on this most of all: it was such a surprising-looking thing that anyone coming face to face with it would be unable to resist touching it to see what it was. With the exception of monkeys and apes, mammals lack opposable thumbs and do not use their sense of touch to identify things they don't recognise. They use their sense of smell instead. Where we touch, they sniff. During the lunch break, I would place the frog on Franck Louvier's desk, right on his Montblanc penholder. Against this black background, its yellow colour would be sure to attract attention. *Phyllobates* are so small and so lethargic that they move very little, not at all like our own European frogs, which can jump around for hours all over the place.

On his return from lunch, Franck Louvier tended to shut himself in his office to make phone calls. I planned to commandeer his two minions for a comprehensive tour of the basement. Sabine would probably be sorting the post then and, on the face of it, would have no reason to disturb him. Franck would step into his office and shut the door ... forever, one might say. Not seeing him come back out, someone would eventually knock and, getting no answer, would open it. And then – surprise! He would be found slumped over his desk. In the ensuing panic, no one would notice the tiny yellow frog measuring less than three centimetres in length. For my part, alerted by the commotion that would inevitably follow, I would hurry upstairs and discreetly recover the *Phyllobates* in a paper handkerchief.

The crime was not without risk. A perfect crime is never truly perfect. It achieves perfection if its low probability of risk is unrealised. What if the frog was discovered? I had no doubt Louvier would prod the frog with his finger, and maybe pick it up by one leg to look at it, but I did not know what he would do next. Perhaps he would throw open his office door and demand to know what the creature was doing there. That was a risk. But, skilled headhunter that I was, what I had discerned of Louvier's psychological make-up so far told me that he was very unlikely to react in that way. He was the last person to fling open his door and call out to everyone within earshot: 'Hey, guess what, guys? There's a fluorescent-yellow frog on my desk; it's tiny! Unbelievable!' No. Rather, he would grab it with a shudder of disgust, while carrying on with his phone conversation, and toss it into the waste-paper basket or perhaps crush it underfoot, without pausing to wonder how it had got there.

And who could have told him that? Only me ...

A packet of Benson & Hedges Gold and a lighter I had taken care to fill with fuel took pride of place on my desk. I had tapped the cigarettes up out of the paper lining and wafted them under my nose. Again, the new pack's characteristic aroma of dry tea and rancid honey made me smile. Before the day was out, I would be able to light up and savour the pleasure.

The morning passed quietly. An ongoing search to fill a post in sustainable development took up a good two hours. I already had three candidates to put forward, but I wanted to locate a fourth, more of an outsider, who might appeal to this quite avant-garde company. I scrutinised the pages of *Les Échos* like a medium, trying to make contact with the current market vibe. A recent flurry of movement in the sector might well cause a ripe apple to drop from its branches. Atalaxia, the group special-ising in the recycling of plastic waste, was likely to be hit hard by its rival Sagemac's IPO. If the manoeuvre was confirmed, my apple might very well drop right into my hand. I was about to call one of my research assistants and ask him to find me the organisation chart for Atalaxia when Véronique pushed open my office door.

'Are you coming to the Bon Coin for lunch?' she asked.

I glanced at my watch: lunchtime already, and I hadn't noticed. I told her I wanted to finish my current search and would join them at the bistro in about fifteen minutes. As soon as she had closed the door behind her, I spun round in my black leather chair to stare at my suit jacket hanging on the coat stand. I had to act now. I felt the adrenaline rush as I got to my feet. My wallet had been replaced by the test tube containing the *Phyllobates*. That morning, I had shut myself in the bathroom to wrap it in an extraordinary quantity of Kleenex, before slipping it into my pocket. It had come to no harm; I had transported it as cautiously as a phial of nitroglycerine.

The corridors were empty. A single photocopier churned in the distance, doubtless an intern copying a folder before heading out to lunch. Lift – fifth floor – the executive offices. The doors opened at the deserted floor. I stole over the fitted carpet, listening out for the slightest noise. Nothing. I pushed the double glass doors that separated the CEO's suite from the rest of the space. Sabine's office was empty. I glanced at the clutter surrounding her computer: small Hello Kitty figurines stood among a litter of multicoloured pens. Her screen showed the same Caribbean beach as mine. I should tell her, I thought, then checked myself: I wasn't supposed to be up here.

I listened out again. Nothing. Not a sound. There was really no one there. To make triply sure, I knocked on the door to the two minions' office. No answer. Then Franck Louvier's door. My knocks were met with silence. The gold letters 'HBC' had been ripped off the varnished wood, but their outline could still be seen. 'Usurper,' I thought, and opened the door.

Hubert Beauchamps-Charellier's office was practically unchanged. The most notable difference was the smell: by some quasi-supernatural phenomenon, the room no longer smelled of anything at all. Yet the aroma of cigars had always wafted within these walls. The smell had disappeared with HBC; it had refused to stick around for his successor. I took a few steps across the cream fitted carpet to the hole made by HBC's last cigar. I knelt to take a closer look: the acrylic fibres had scorched, then melted, leaving a slightly shiny black crust. I touched it cautiously, like a wound. I needed to feel the burn under my fingers, like St Thomas touching the wound in Christ's side. Franck Louvier had tried to call someone in to replace the carpet almost immediately, but the office had stood its ground: the first fitter, then the second, and finally the third had all replied that they were fully booked for the next two months. Sabine had told me that. The smell had disappeared, but the carpet refused to be pulled up. Stepping into a dead man's shoes is never a good idea, especially if they're far too big.

The large polished-mahogany desktop was empty apart from a few luxury accessories: a gold Cartier carriage clock, a penholder and a silver Montblanc pen, a pencil pot bearing the emblem of the Harvard Alumni Association, a state-of-the-art flat screen and one of the latest generation of tactile keyboards. Louvier's screen saver was a kind of luminous fractal form that regenerated itself endlessly, turning over and over in the void. There was a paperweight formed from a sort of X shape in a metal circle on a marble base. I had no idea what the symbol meant, but found it vaguely fascinating: it suited him.

My Rolex showed twelve minutes past one. I removed the test tube from my pocket, took a last look at the *Phyllobates*, motionless at the bottom, then opened the top. Majortom888 had sealed it in the proper way, neither pushed in too far, nor too little. I slipped the cork back into my pocket, took out a Kleenex and tapped the tube, tipping it towards the desktop. A little Colombian water dripped out and then *Phyllobates* slid gently down the glass onto the paper handkerchief. With a thousand precautions, I moved it over to the base of the penholder, until it deigned to extend a cautious leg, then another, and pull itself up onto the shiny black surface. With the rolled tip of my Kleenex, I pushed it slightly to make sure it was right in the middle of the rectangle. Obligingly, the frog shifted a little. I stood back. The effect was striking: a tiny fluorescent-yellow frog against a black background. No doubt about it, the first person to see it would prod it with their finger.

'You stay right there,' I told it, wagging an admonishing forefinger.

And I left the room.

'Are we going to be down here for much longer, Monsieur?'

'As long as it takes,' I replied, drily.

The basement at HBC had been disused for more than twelve years and no one cleaned or dusted here now. Only the concierge unlocked the door from time to time to deposit an old computer, or a set of shelves no one needed. This was where Franck Louvier planned to install my new office, down in the dust with all the useless, outdated pieces of equipment: the perfect metaphor. The timed light switches were no longer working and the three of us moved around by the light of torches carried by the two yes-men. I had requisitioned them on their return from lunch. They weren't overly excited to follow me down into the semi-darkness and the cobwebs, but they had no choice. I was playing my part to the hilt, wandering through the rooms, tape measure in hand, stepping over upturned desks and chairs, then calling out the measurements: 'Seven metres wide! Four metres long! Two metres thirty headroom!' They noted everything down meticulously, one holding his torch over the other's note-book. Idiots.

I pushed the door to another room and found myself twenty-five years back in time. This was the office in which I had begun my career at HBC. The furniture was little altered, the metal storage cabinet was still in its old place, the shelves too. The swivel chair with its brown fabric cover had been mine. No one had ever replaced it.

'I think I'm going to choose this room,' I said quietly.

'But it's not the biggest, Monsieur!' said one of the other two.

'It's my decision, not yours,' I told him, walking over to the cupboard.

I tried to open it by turning the handle, but it was jammed: not locked, but the metal had probably warped. Annoyed by the sudden resistance, I leaned against it hard until it yielded with a loud clang of metal. It was full of folders. Old folders written in biro. I dusted them off with the flat of my hand. 'Beauchamps-Charellier – Profiles – 1982', the year I joined the firm. 'Strategy Report' by Jean Jacquard. I recognised his fine handwriting and his mania for using carbon copies, already outdated at the time. The ex-screenwriter had his quirks. One of the folders had a heading that was completely out of place: 'Michael Philips Production'.

'Give me a light,' I said.

One of the boys passed me his torch. I shone it on the old folder, which was typewritten and dated 1977. It didn't make sense that it was there in one of the firm's filing cabinets. The old contract was drafted in English. I couldn't decipher it all, but two names reappeared again and again: Steven Spielberg and François Truffaut, and the title, in English: *Close Encounters of the Third Kind*. According to the document, Jacquard had contributed to the writing of the sequences featuring Truffaut. So that was it, his American period with a star director that I had heard about at the time. The title was strangely resonant: what did we do in our business if not encounter people, forever hoping that the third one on the list would be the rare pearl? The connection between the art of cinema and our own was more obvious than it might at first seem. Tucked in amongst the dozens of sheets relating to the film, I found a black-and-white photograph of a man with a birdlike face and a smouldering look: the actor Charles Denner. The file was becoming stranger still. I turned the picture over. On the back, in purple ink, Jacquard had written 'the ladies' man?'.

But my discoveries ended there: one of the men's phones rang and he answered it straight away.

'Oh my God!' he cried out.

I turned to him, then shone the torch on my Rolex. Twenty-seven minutes past two.

The doors to the fifth floor opened to the sound of piercing cries. They came from Sabine. For the second time in her life, the poor woman had opened her boss's door to find him dead. Sabine was 'totally out of it' as my daughter would have said. It was impossible to make her stop. As soon as she had finished one scream, she caught her breath and began over again, louder. A few headhunters who specialised in marketing roles stood watching her, transfixed. The sound was penetrating, like a car alarm. We might almost have got used to it. At the far end of the corridor, Gold arrived, looking distraught, followed by Véronique. One of the two yes-men lost his nerve. He rushed over to Sabine, gripped her by the shoulders and shook her hard.

'What the fuck's happened?' he yelled.

Sabine's shriek died in her throat and she stared at us, wild-eyed, before bursting into tears, as if our looks were somehow accusatory. Weakly, she lifted a trembling finger and pointed to Franck Louvier's office door. Véronique was the first to reach it. She stood on the threshold.

'Oh fuck,' she breathed. 'I'll call the emergency services.'

Gold pushed everyone aside and walked into the office, knelt beside Louvier, took his hand, and pressed two fingers against his neck. Véronique picked up Sabine's phone. Poor Sabine was sitting at her desk now, staring at her Hello Kitty figurines with empty eyes.

'Jean, what do I tell them?' yelled Véronique.

'Tell them he's dead,' said Gold, flatly.

My turn to enter the office. Sabine must have suffered an appalling shock: Louvier was lying in exactly the same spot as HBC. The perfect remake.

Everyone gathered around Sabine's desk. Now she was repeating that it wasn't her fault, she'd had nothing to do with it, but no one was listening. I felt in my pocket for my pack of Benson & Hedges Gold and my lighter, and moved closer to the body. I took out a cigarette and clicked the lighter. The tobacco caught. First drag. The nicotine in my lungs released endorphins like the lava plug of a volcano blowing sky-high. The divine molecules raced through my blood at the speed of light. Serene calm broke over me like a wave. My legs would no longer carry me and I squatted down.

'Fabrice, this really isn't the time!' said Gold, crossly.

I turned to him. He was standing in the doorframe. I could hardly see him. At the sight of my enemy's body, my eyes had filled with tears of joy. The doctor with the emergency team diagnosed a sudden, devastating heart attack.

'Did he practise any sport?' he asked.

'He swam like a bloody fish,' said Verider, chewing a Vichy Pastille.

He had said nothing until now, astounded that his dream had come true so soon.

'He went to the gym, too,' said one of the yes-men.

'His heart gave out ...' said the doctor, solemnly.

No one had thought to search the waste-paper basket, from which I recovered, unnoticed, a yellow Post-it note and a yellow frog. In the toilets, I slipped it back into its tube. The frog glided gently down to its mossy bed and I replaced the gauze and cork.

'Mission accomplished, my little beauty,' I congratulated it, as I returned the tube to my inside jacket pocket.

Back in my office, I took out another cigarette and lit it. Again, the intoxicating pleasure enveloped me. Then, shortly after, I came back down to earth. Nothing. All my personal dials were back at zero. For the scientific record, I can state that the change in a person's alphas and betas after committing an act of murder lasts almost an hour.

Phyllobates terribilis had joined me in the highly select circle of those who have committed a murder. I couldn't reconcile myself to the idea of abandoning my accomplice-for-a-day in a hermetically sealed bag or burning her in the fireplace. Passing discreetly over her criminal record, I would find her a new home, bigger and better than her test tube. A small ad on the Herpetomania forum brought me into contact a few days later with another frog enthusiast. I met him briefly at lunchtime in a bistro not far from the Bon Coin. I handed over the test tube, but asked for no payment in exchange.

'The money doesn't matter,' I said. 'I'm leaving to take up an important new post abroad and I can't take my animals with me. Take good care of her,' I told him.

He told me she'd have a terrarium measuring half a cubic metre all to herself, stocked with perfectly adapted flora. My murderous frog would serve out her sentence in a luxury prison and her jailer would lavish her with care and attention. A few weeks later, my own destiny would match that of the golden poison frog's: murder and a comfortable cage, as befits rare specimens like us.

Had my curious invented pretext – 'I'm leaving to take up an important new post abroad' – reached divine ears? 'Abroad' in my case was no further afield than the fifth floor of HBC Consulting, but the important new post part was perfectly accurate. Fate redressed her injustice.

The board, based at La Défense, contacted me the morning after Franck Louvier's death. I was invited at my earliest convenience to the fifty-seventh floor of the Topaze Tower, where I learned that the shareholders and their representatives had been fully aware of HBC's wishes for his succession. What had led them to ignore his preference? It's one of the great mysteries of business strategy: people take the wrong decision, at the wrong time, yet they remain convinced they're doing the right thing. Analysis, advice, experience, nothing will dissuade them. Suddenly, a bizarre turn of events will cause a group at the height of its glory to fall as surely as a dead leaf in autumn. And these senseless mistakes are not confined to the financial world. The most famous example in civilian life concerns a maritime manoeuvre that has gone down in history: the decision of the captain of the *Titanic*, who ordered his ship into reverse ten minutes too late. Yet all the eyewitness accounts agree that his first officers had informed him of the presence of a huge iceberg straight ahead. He had assured them everything was fine; they would sail past it. As the whole world saw. The dizzying collapses of Vivendi and Enron, the bursting of the Internet bubble, all showed how taking a bad decision and sticking to it can push an organisation to the brink in just a few months. Now, HBC Consulting had had the intelligence to go into reverse, not ten minutes late but after one death too many, dare I say.

'You'll be taking over as CEO of HBC Consulting, in accordance with the express wishes of Hubert Beauchamps-Charellier. Monsieur Valantine, you have full executive powers and our complete confidence.'

I rose and bowed my head to applause from all around the table.

'I'll do my best to continue in the spirit of Hubert Beauchamps-Charellier,' I said. 'Thank you.'

Twenty-four hours later, the news landed on my colleagues' desks and I took up my post that same day. I decided to summon everyone to the purple room in order to give a short, simple speech, paying tribute to our founder and setting us back on course in the best tradition of the firm. I wondered if Gold and Véronique might feel a touch of jealousy at my appointment. I knew human nature only too well – the lure of ambition, financial gain, a thirst for recognition. One person's success was not always met with universal joy. But I need not have feared. When I came across Véronique in the lobby, she kissed me on both cheeks and congratulated me heartily. Her display of affection took me by surprise, then my eyes fell on the silver chain she wore around her neck. There was a new addition to her usual charms and pendants: a grey baroque pearl. I understood then that her delight was not due to my new-found status. I could have become President of the United States and she would have greeted the news in precisely the same way. Her nascent love affair with Jean Gold had eclipsed everything.

And what of my own love life in the excitement of these new developments? Sidonie clasped me tightly in her arms when she heard the news. She laid her head on my shoulder for a long time, in the silence of the sitting room, then said: 'You deserve it. You're a good man, Fabrice.'

There was a solemnity in her voice, a hint of gravity and nostalgia. I should have liked her to cheer enthusiastically, pop the cork on a bottle of Dom Pérignon, and for us both to get drunk while raising our glasses to the photo of Francis Bacon. My success seemed to trouble the one person I had not thought of: my wife.

Having said a firm 'thank you and goodbye' to the two yes-men, I took possession of my new office and replaced Hubert Beauchamps-Charellier's chair with the one that had faced it until now. A subtle exchange, based on pure superstition. The mahogany desktop was spotless and smelled of wax polish. I arranged my things: the photograph of Sidonie with Andy Warhol, her favourite picture; one of my daughter before her ludicrous hairstyle; a crystal ashtray; seashells brought back from holiday; and a gold Dunhill table lighter. The smoking ban was in force throughout the building, but I was now safe in the last bastion of resistance. But this fortunate state of affairs was of no use to me whatsoever, because the pleasure had vanished once again. Would this feeling of being punished stay with me for the rest of my life? According to the magician in the fruit and vegetable section at Rungis market, the only person who could reverse what he had done was Di Caro himself, and he was in prison. In custody, awaiting trial, at which he was likely to be sentenced to two or three years inside if the cop with the mirrored shades was to be believed. Would I be able to hold out that long? In light of subsequent events, I can confidently state here that, no, I could not.

Sometimes, life hands you a truly wonderful moment on a plate. A small gift from the Almighty or an exquisite treat from some playful angelic tempter. These unexpected shafts of sunlight take the most varied forms: a lovely young woman in a sheer dress on a café terrace reading the same book as you – a chance opportunity to engage her in conversation. A friend you'd lost touch with for years who appears at the gate to a long-haul flight and with whom you chat throughout the journey. A neighbour you detest who decides to reseal his window frames one sunny day, standing on his balcony rail, fifteen metres above the ground. This last gift presented itself to me one Saturday afternoon.

Two days before, I had seen the wife of Pascal Brunet, my charming neighbour from building B, staircase C, in the main hallway. She was being wheeled out on a stretcher, her face bruised and swollen, and the emergency team were telling her that she must lie still.

'I fell down a staircase,' she told me, in a thick voice.

'There are no stairs in your apartment, Madame,' said a paramedic, categorically.

'Down the main staircase, in the building,' she insisted, weakly.

'Of course, of course …' said the paramedic, who was no fool.

He caught my eye and laid his hand on my arm.

'Could we speak to you for a second?' he asked politely, but firmly.

He led me down the corridor.

'Are you one of this woman's neighbours?'

'Yes,' I nodded, uncomfortably.

'Then you'll know what this is all about,' he said. 'You need to call a social worker because, one day, your neighbour ... Well, we'll be wheeling her out on a stretcher, but she won't be making excuses any more, if you see what I mean.'

'I see,' I said, gravely.

'So you'll remember to do that?' he said, patting me quickly on the shoulder.

Manly comradeship.

It was the weekend. I was alone in the apartment, with nothing particular to do. Sidonie had gone in to the *Moderna* office to put the finishing touches to the layouts for the next edition. As I wandered through the empty rooms, an iced *pastis* in one hand, my eyes fell on the mirror in the hallway. Over the years, Sidonie and I had tucked photographs into the frame: Emma as a baby, then a toddler, then a young girl, along with pictures from our own childhoods – Sidonie as a little girl, standing on top of a sandcastle, on a swing, in a pool with her inflatable armbands. My eye fell on a photograph of me, as a child, in the Tuileries Garden. My hair, which later turned dark brown and then grey, had been blond then. I was standing by the pool with the little sailing boats, smiling into the camera. I held a toy: a multi-coloured windmill. I looked joyously happy, like a Walt Disney bunny. Gazing into the little boy's eyes, I asked him: could you possibly know that forty years later, you'd smoke two packets of cigarettes a day and become a murderer? The little boy had no answer. A curious nostalgia gripped my heart: I wanted to go back to that afternoon, with my multicoloured windmill. It seemed as if that day in the Tuileries back in the sixties might have been the best day of my life. Winston Churchill had expressed just that feeling in a famous phrase but I couldn't remember it exactly.

Emma would be home that evening from Barcelona. I would be sure to ask her if she had kept her promise, but, in reality, I wasn't much bothered. Emma could tell me whatever she liked, it was a lost battle from the outset. I went back to the kitchen intending to pour myself another pastis. Through the half-open window, I heard the sound of sawing and swearing. I went to look. My neighbour was replacing the pane of glass he had broken the other night. At the same time, he was scraping out the putty from all the other panes and preparing to replace it. He was clearly one of those Sunday DIY enthusiasts who spend their entire weekend with a hammer in their hand, rather than paying attention to their wife. Though on second thoughts, my neighbour would have done better to spend entire weeks at his DIY ... I saw the poor woman's face again as she was wheeled out on the trolley by the emergency team. She was still in hospital. How could anyone strike a woman? Their own wife? I had never once thought to raise my hand to Sidonie. My blood ran cold at the very idea. I leaned on our balcony rail and watched him. He was sturdily built, but quite short, brown-haired, about forty or forty-five. He was finding it hard to reach to the topmost panes and, rather than stand on a stool, he had put one foot on the balcony rail and hoisted himself up, keeping one hand on the window frame. With the other, he was gouging out the old putty with a chisel. He was scraping rhythmically, like an insect – a termite working hard to hollow out a plank of wood. A small, bright, white spot flickered on the wall above the window.

It was a few seconds before I realised it was coming from my watch face, which had caught the sun and projected a spot of light onto the opposite wall, like the little red dot tracking a target in the telescopic sight of a rifle in an action movie. Impact. Death. My spot was bigger and white. I amused myself by moving it down the window. If I shifted my wrist by the tiniest fraction, the spot would suddenly drop several centimetres. It was a delicate manoeuvre. The circle reached his denim shirt. Gently, I ran it along his arm, then followed the direction of his neck, slowly, carefully, as far as his cheek, then his left eye.

'Hey! Go and play with that somewhere else!' he barked, twisting his head to look in my direction.

I spread my arms wide in a gesture of apology. He carried on scraping. My urge for a second pastis had vanished now. Another had taken its place.

'I feel like smoking a cigarette,' I told him.

'What the hell's that got to do with me?' he answered, not bothering to look round.

'I can think of a way to get you involved,' I whispered to myself.

I took my cigarettes and lighter out of my pocket and left them on the kitchen table before turning away from the window and walking into the hallway. One by one, I removed all the photographs from the mirror and placed them on the chest of drawers. Firmly, I unhooked the mirror from its nail. It was heavier than I had anticipated, but not too heavy for what I planned to do. Back in the kitchen, I placed the mirror on the worktop and glanced at the window. My termite was still tap-tap-tapping at his putty, perched on his balcony rail, leaning against the window frame. No need to call a social worker. Noiselessly, carefully, I took the mirror over to the window and lodged it so that it faced the sun.

'Hey!' I called out.

He turned his head to look over at me. Instantly, sharply, I pivoted the mirror. The flash blinded him. The chisel slipped on the putty, he reached his hand out to catch it, and his whole body tumbled after it into the void.

'Didn't you hear him fall?'

'No, I was watching TV,' I told Sidonie, exhaling smoke.

From Emma's bedroom window, Sidonie and I stood watching as, down in the courtyard, the emergency team prepared to shift the body onto a stretcher, while a police officer made notes. I looked for the young paramedic who had suggested I call a social worker, but didn't see him. The neighbour's body had left a pool of blood on the paving stones. The police officer took a few digital photographs of the ground, the blood, and the balcony as seen from below. In the neighbour's apartment, one of the emergency team was closing the window with the missing pane. He spoke to the building's concierge; I saw their lips moving behind the glass. My blood surged in my veins. The pleasure. The pleasure of smoking and, perhaps, of killing, too. Soon, it would be an hour since Pascal Brunet had smashed into the floor of the courtyard. This cigarette would be one of the last before the curfew came down and the lights of pleasure were extinguished.

'You're smoking a lot. I thought you didn't enjoy it any more,' said Sidonie.

'Sometimes I do; it comes back,' I said mysteriously.

She didn't pursue the subject, and closed the window, saying enough was enough and we weren't going to waste any tears over a bastard like him. I nodded, saying nothing. She went into the hallway to fetch the shopping bag she had left there when she came home.

'Did you move the photos around on the mirror?' she asked.

'Yes, I cleaned the glass,' I said, expecting some sort of response.

Nothing. Sidonie returned from the hallway with the shopping.

'I stopped in at Dalloyau,' she said, putting the bag on the worktop.

I looked at her. Who would imagine I had anything whatever to do with the neighbour's fall? 'Anyone can commit the perfect crime,' I thought.

That evening, we ate dinner with Emma, back from Barcelona with a golden tan. She admitted that she hadn't stopped smoking while she was away, but had cut down. Her broken promise didn't prompt any reprimands in particular, because, in truth, we were pleased to see our daughter with a normal haircut: the dreadlocks had disappeared; her hair was sleek once again, and much shorter. Her make-up was more discreet, too. As Sidonie commented, when we were getting ready for bed: 'I think Benjamin has been a good influence.'

It was quite possible we were through the worst of her adolescent crisis, which had started two years previously. But the dinner was not without its awkward moments, nonetheless. Inevitably, Emma pointed out to us that the tapas in Barcelona were much better than 'stuff from Dalloyau'. To which Sidonie replied that she could get to work in the kitchen and make some for us to try.

'Absolutely, we'd love that,' I added.

Immediately, Emma acted the victim: everything she said got twisted around and turned against her; we were both ganging up one her. Her teenage crisis was perhaps in the descendant, but she had a few more cards up her sleeve: provocative scraps like her story of a walk they had taken in a red-light district of Barcelona, and her detailed description of the accessories they had bought in a sex shop.

'So? What about it? Don't come over all shocked; Maman organised an entire exhibition full of giant penises last year,' she objected.

Sidonie raised her eyes to the ceiling. The show had featured conceptual works by an artist who explored the nature of form, she explained crossly, nothing at all to do with sex toys.

'They were still, like, gigantic vibrators,' said Emma, further goading her mother.

'Perhaps we could change the subject?' I asked coldly, hoping to turn the conversation back to the Sagrada Família.

Another provocative act had displeased Sidonie greatly. Over pre-dinner drinks, Emma had raised her glass of port to 'that bastard neighbour who just got splattered'. Sidonie asked her to change her tone immediately, and not to talk ill of the dead.

Regarding my new status at HBC, my daughter's response was entirely in keeping with the chief concerns of her age group: 'Cool, you'll be earning, like, ten times more!'

A holiday. My many recent life changes had given me the urge to get away for a while. The frustrated smoker needed a rest, the dedicated manager prescribed some time out, the accomplished murderer was calling for an intermission. Three personas in one were asking for a break. Leaders Need a Break: the phrase sounded like the refrain of some obscure English pop song, but in reality it was the name of one of the world's most secretive exclusive travel agencies. As the newly appointed head of HBC Consulting, I had access to the account and to Hubert Beauchamps-Charellier's password. Leaders Need a Break functioned like a kind of private club: each of its members, scattered across the five continents, paid a vast annual subscription in exchange for which they could at any time choose a destination and the perks that came with it. My first visit to the website made my head spin. I had expected luxury package holidays, but not on this scale.

The Caribbean Silence Break offered a vast villa, built entirely of pale wood, raised on stilts overlooking the waters of a private lagoon, accessible only by boat or helicopter. A staff of ten – including a fisherman and cleaners – were on hand to cater to the client's every whim. The price of the trip wasn't given nor that of any of the extras, which ranged from scuba diving to hang-gliding. Members of the organisation paid nothing; they simply had to log on, then indicate their chosen start date and the length of their stay. If my daughter could have two weeks in Barcelona, I could go ahead and plan an absolutely breathtaking summer holiday with Sidonie. A perfect and very welcome surprise.

Another package – Luxury Ice Storm – offered a stay in a private residence on the edge of the Arctic Circle, with an incredible range of services plus a pool, sauna, jacuzzi and outings to view the polar ice. There were uninterrupted views over a glacier lagoon, a weekend in an igloo, with snowmobile rides, a discovery hike to meet 'our cousins, the seals', in partnership with the not-for-profit organisation Greenplanet. A helicopter flight over the bay. The photographs of the bedrooms and sitting room, with its views over the ice, looked like something out of a science-fiction movie.

The Venezia Island Vivaldi Break took guests to a private island close to Venice. Boatmen, domestic staff, a head chef, museum guides, a gondolier and gardeners were on hand throughout your stay. The palatial residence, running the length of the island, featured an underground pool built to resemble a natural cave, a private cinema and an observatory complete with telescope, for star-gazing. Paintings by Guardi and Canaletto hung on the walls, and the site did not specify whether they were originals or copies; anything seemed possible. At the bottom of the page, an icon indicated that the trip had already been taken. I looked at the pictures of the manicured lawns and knew that Hubert Beauchamps-Charellier had walked there, doubtless in the company of Pierre, whom we had glimpsed so briefly at the apartment on Rue Jacob.

The Nautilus Luxury Break gave clients the opportunity to get away from it all three hundred metres below the waves, in the Bahamas. The private residence was accessible only via submersible. The bubble-shaped windows afforded views of sea life and the blue ocean depths. A personal chef prepared dishes of shark and squid like no one else on Earth. The building's oval shapes and Plexiglas bubbles put me in mind of my father's architectural schemes; the luxury underwater home might have sprung from the pages of one of his notebooks.

The list went on, but I didn't have time to look at every page on the site. I was expected at a working lunch with the second-in-command of a well-known automobile group. He was a long-standing client and the informal meeting was designed to strengthen our ties and reassure him in the wake of HBC's death. All things considered, the Caribbean villa on stilts seemed the best summer destination. I saved the page and sent a link to my personal email. I would open it in front of Sidonie that evening, over aperitifs.

Two minutes past seven. The daylight seemed to have faded, and yet it wasn't late. In recent years, the approach of summer had been marked by weather phenomena such as this, heralding a downpour of tropical proportions. The light would turn a kind of sandy yellow, filtering through great grey masses of cloud while bright flashes lit them from below. Sheet lightning. The business lunch had gone well. The pleasant second-in-command of the major automobile group had presented me with a silver paperweight depicting their latest factory. It was extremely heavy and I had placed it on my desk beside the photograph of Sidonie with Andy Warhol. I considered taking it home, but the gift would amuse no one but me, and I had something far better to offer: my Caribbean Silence Break, the perfect morsel to savour with our aperitifs.

The apartment was bathed in the same lugubrious yellow light. The lights were all out, but the door wasn't double-locked.

'Are you here?' I called into the silence.

In the sitting room, Sidonie snapped on the little lamp next to the fireplace. She was half reclining on the sofa. She looked at me for a few seconds, then said quietly: 'I'm here.'

'Are you feeling ill?'

'No.'

I took off my navy raincoat and set down my briefcase in the hallway. I felt overcome by a sudden sense – a certainty – of danger. There was something abnormal in the darkness, in

Sidonie's 'I'm here.' Something was wrong. I had felt it since her return from New York, something undefined, misty, pervasive. There was something the matter. Alone in the hallway, I felt like a man facing the sea, waiting for a giant wave to break over me. Yes, that was exactly the feeling. When I entered the sitting room, the atmosphere was more oppressive still. Sidonie was wearing her black Saint-Laurent suit and a fine-knit white sweater. Her black bobbed hair seemed to gleam with the same bluish sheen as her suit. Her eyes followed me around the room, and there was an infinite sadness in her gaze, something palpable that turned the couple of metres between us into a vast, unconquerable distance. For a moment, I even suffered the optical illusion that she was a very long way away, as if my eyes were struggling to make out the contours of her face and to recognise her.

'Fabrice, there's something I need to tell you ...' she said.

I heard the muffled roar of the approaching wave: something was about to hit me hard, I could tell. But what? What could possibly hit me that hard? Even as I asked myself the question, a faint light began to flash on and off in my subconscious. My personal Achilles heel was about to play me the most devastating trick of my life: I understood nothing about modern art and, at a more basic level, I didn't like it. It was the manufacturing fault in my relationship with Sidonie. Over the years, the faulty component had reached breaking point and given way, and bringing everything to a halt. That was the meaning of the silence, the yellow gloom. Something had stopped.

'Sit down,' she said quietly.

I sat down. We looked at one another but said nothing. I raised my eyebrows, inviting her to speak. She closed her eyes then opened them again suddenly.

'Fabrice, I can't lie. There's someone else in my life.'

The moment of impact. I sat motionless. The wave broke over me; I could feel its weight bearing down on me. I sensed its speed and the crushing effect all at once. Something enormous that will sweep you away if you make the slightest movement. I stayed completely still.

'I don't know whether we should split up or not. I don't know what to do. But I can't pretend. I can't invent stories: non-existent cocktails, non-existent meetings at the magazine. That's not what I want.'

I could find no words. Not a single sentence. My mind felt oddly empty, like a hard disk scrubbed of its data. I think I could have sat like that for hours, even days, but one question fought its way out: 'Who is it?'

Sidonie exhaled almost imperceptibly through her nose, then her dimples deepened slightly, signalling her discomfort. Her answer was slow in coming, and I asked again, 'Who is it?'

'It's Damon Bricker,' she snapped, at last.

Moscow, December 1957

It was cold that winter and the onion domes of Red Square were topped with snow. It wasn't my first time in the country; my previous visits had been low-key – just checking on our list of friends and giving them their mailing instructions, or the new telephone numbers they could reach us on. One of them, Natasha – known as Tasha – invited me into her modest apartment in a building overlooking a small square whose name I don't recall. They held a market there every Friday. Old ladies in headscarves came to sell vegetables. They were fat, with ruddy cheeks. I remember we bought some cabbage and Tasha made soup. The soup was real bad, and we added some butter to the water. I know all you little ones are bored by small details like this! But your dear old grandpa remembers them all as clear as day. The butter came in a blue wrapper and Tasha translated the characters I couldn't manage to read. We spent a good month that way; the neighbours didn't get suspicious. I grew a beard to make me look more Russian, and I dressed in Russian clothes that Tasha had bought at a market before I got there. If anyone greeted me, I would nod respectfully but I never opened my mouth. If anyone asked about me, Tasha would say I was her fiancé, and that I was just back from Siberia where I'd been working on a military base. I was on leave until I was posted someplace else. I didn't have a lot to say, but I was a good man. That was enough for the neighbours, who in any case were not keen on getting mixed up in other folks' business. The less they knew about it, the better. In Cold War Moscow, people's natural curiosity melted away like the snow, you might say. I had a love affair with Tasha; she was very pretty, and she worked as a waitress in a restaurant. Hiding behind my cover, I made my investigations. I was alone in the city. I had been provided with papers, and a disability card that stated I was mute. It proved useful on two occasions when soldiers spoke to me in Russian. I showed them my card. I was a pretty good mute. During one of the checks, they burst out laughing and made jokes I didn't understand.

The Vladimir apartment building was a private condo that was home to five Communist Party executives. The man I was interested in, whom we called Sergei, though that wasn't his real name, lived on the first floor. I had been given a duplicate set of his keys. Locks were so much simpler back then! Two of the simplest keys you could imagine to open one door. It's all so much harder nowadays, what with electronics and codes and whatnot, but that's a whole other story ... So, I went to the Vladimir building several times, alone, to see what kind of surveillance was in place there. Two guards took it in turns at the main entrance, but they were kind of lazy and they often showed up late. That old Soviet Union we were all so scared of also had its weak points. The men were bored; they preferred to drink vodka and talk in the bar along the street rather than stand there in the snow for hour after hour. I could understand that. Nobody watched the other door, at the back; it opened onto a wash house and a yard where all the residents dried their laundry. There were stairs down to a cellar, and stairs going up to the other floors. That was the door they should have been watching! And that was the way your favourite old grandpa used to go, to get in. My mission was to kill that mean old Sergei, because he'd ordered the elimination of two of our friends in Czechoslovakia. I had to make sure it didn't look like an execution. No weapons! No knives, no gun, no rifle with a telescopic sight. No! Had to make it look like it was an accident. And I couldn't use a car to run the bad guy down either: cars were too complicated.

So, here's what your old grandpa – or your old great-grandpa for you littlest ones – did: I remembered a system that one of the intelligence operatives had told me about during the Normandy landings. He said they'd used it in Chicago during Prohibition, to eliminate a mafia guy who was trading in liquor. I checked out every inch of Sergei's apartment, then I told Tasha to buy me the exact same light bulbs as the ones I'd seen in his chandelier. After that, I used a real fine diamond drill to make a hole in each bulb. Just a teeny little hole. And once I'd pierced a hole in my six light bulbs, because there were six of them on the chandelier, I took a syringe and I used it to draw the gasoline from out of a can and inject it into the light bulbs, through the holes I'd drilled. 'Bout three fluid ounces, or a third of a cup of gasoline in each bulb. Then I used a piece of Scotch tape to seal up each of the holes.

Question from Jordan (age 6): Did Tasha buy the Scotch tape?

Answer from Grandpa Edward: Yup, little fella, that's a real smart question! I can see you're going to go far! Tasha did buy the Scotch tape. So I had six light bulbs filled with gasoline and sealed back up. I wrapped them in pieces of cloth and placed them very carefully in a briefcase, and went back to the Vladimir building when Sergei wasn't at home. I went in by the back door which still had nobody watching it, and used my set of keys to get into the apartment. I replaced all the light bulbs in the chandelier with my own, and left.

When Sergei came home, he would turn on the light in the hallway first, and then the dining room and, lastly, the chandelier in the sitting room, and ... *Ka-boom!* The whole thing would blow up, a huge fire would start right there and, in just a few seconds, the gasoline would spatter all over the place and whoever had switched on the lights would be covered in it if he was standing near the chandelier!

So, what was supposed to happen, happened, and next day all the papers were talking about the fire in the Vladimir building that had claimed one victim – Sergei – and had almost destroyed all the other floors. But, luckily, the firefighters got there in time. The perfect accident – because everyone thought the fire had been started by an electrical fault. It was an old building, an accident was entirely plausible. And once everything had been drenched in water by the firefighters, it was a total mess and there was no trace of any gasoline left!

See attached Grandpa Edward's own diagram of how to make the light bulbs.

Long live freedom, my darling young ones!

As I walked through the labyrinthine DIY basement at the BHV department store, one of my father's phrases popped into my head: 'People always end up doing what they're best at.' To which he would add, with a sardonic smile: 'And since I'm good at nothing, that's what I do,' before disappearing into a cloud of smoke. A series of puffs. Silence. Face set in a tragic mask. And what if my greatest talent was committing murder? Murder as the logical culmination, the summit of my abilities. The metaphorical manhunting I had practised for over twenty years had become real. I was proving a formidable predator. Just as the lowly research assistant I had once been, had proved himself one of the best manhunters in the firm.

There was a dizzying array of tools. I walked through the different sections, seeing dozens of manual or electric sanders, each with its own special purpose; saws, and hammers; nails and nuts by the hundred. There was a deceptively laid-back air about the place, but in reality it was aimed strictly at semi-professionals who knew everything about the uses and handling of the items on display. Once past the sandpaper section, I found the electric drills, at last. The section assistant, a grey-haired man with a luxuriant moustache, was peering closely at a steel drill bit under a spotlight. He held it at arm's length and closed his left eye.

'It's buckled.'

'Are you sure?' asked the bit's owner.

'Sure,' he confirmed.

'So that's why the panel slipped,' said the other man, earnestly, as if he had finally found the solution to some long-standing mystery.

'It's the only possible explanation,' said the moustachioed man, gravely.

The two men looked at one another like conspirators who can say nothing more for fear of being overheard.

'I'll need a new one,' said the customer.

'A twelve?'

'Exactly. I'll have to start all over again,' he said briskly. 'But I'll finish that bookcase if it's the last thing I do!'

Weeks, maybe even months, of Sunday drilling lay before him. I felt a kind of affection for these men, with their passion for DIY, each project a new and peculiarly private challenge. The customer had doubtless decided to make his own reproduction of an antique bookcase, devoting all his energies, every free afternoon, every night to the task, if that was what it took. Failure was not an option. His bookcase had become an end in itself. It's an inherently human characteristic. People set themselves challenges, mountains to climb, oceans to cross, planets to conquer. This gentleman's horizons were less expansive: a piece of furniture for his sitting room, made by his own hand. A challenge on his own modest scale, and already it seemed beyond him.

The section assistant returned with the bit and held it out to the customer, who studied it from every possible angle. Then he asked me what I was looking for, and I explained that I needed a drill capable of piercing a hole in a very thin piece of glass.

'What sort of surface?'

'A light bulb.'

The moustachioed man stared at me hard and raised his right eyebrow. I have no idea how he did it without moving his left eyebrow, too; I've never managed it.

'Why a light bulb?'

In order to head off the hundreds of questions that threatened, I used a technique I had used before and gave an answer so unexpected that it cut off any further discussion.

'I'm a magician; it's for a trick,' I told him.

'Ah!' the man exclaimed. 'I see, in that case,' he added.

He saw nothing at all, but that was fine by me. He turned to his customer, who had stood listening intently to our exchange.

'Monsieur Isidore?'

Delighted to be consulted, the customer turned to me with a broad smile.

'Have you ever had to drill a tiny pinhole?' I asked.

'Ha! Don't talk to me about that!' Monsieur Isidore replied.

He told us how he had pierced holes in the pendants of a crystal chandelier whose hooks were broken. It was impossible to find the old-style hooks, because the piece was eighteenth-century, he said. He had had to use a diamond drill and enlarge the holes in 123 brilliant-cut chandelier pendants, under the fierce gaze of his wife, who was terrified one of them might break. The chandelier was an heirloom she prized more than anything I listened to them talking and decided that DIY enthusiasts were a distinct sub-species. If I hadn't coughed to remind them I was there, they might happily have spent the entire afternoon swapping anecdotes about their respective exploits and adventures in the land of ultra-fine electric drills.

'A light bulb, you say ...'

Monsieur Isidore thought hard, his eyes fixed on a distant point somewhere above the ceiling. Would the DIY fairies whisper the answer in his ear?

'A Dremel,' he said, glancing at the section assistant for approval.

The moustachioed one nodded with satisfaction.

'Good idea! Follow me.'

I followed him through the sections, and Monsieur Isidore came too. A customer stopped him with a question about a Black & Decker random orbital sander with integral dust bag.

'I'm with a customer,' replied the moustachioed man. 'Ask my young colleague here.' He indicated a youth standing nearby, busy grinning at a sales girl.

We reached the section and he took down a black plastic box with a magnificent photograph of the object in question on its lid, under the cellophane wrap.

'Now, let's see: "Dremel, the finest in the range …"' he read. '"Ideal for the smallest jobs: fine metalwork, glasswork, engraving. Full set of ten bits in all diameters gives precision control".'

'*Precision control,*' breathed Monsieur Isidore, raising an index finger.

The idea seemed to excite him.

'"The conical carbon-diamond tip drills all materials. Diameters between two and four millimetres. Optimal precision. Anti-vibration. Perfect for all your delicate work." You won't find better than this,' the sales assistant concluded, handing me the box.

I thanked him warmly and shook Monsieur Isidore by the hand. He was unable to resist asking me what the trick involved.

'It's a disappearing trick, of sorts,' I said, evasively.

'A magician will never reveal his secrets!' said the man with the moustache. 'Now then, that twelve-millimetre bit?' He returned to Monsieur Isidore.

'Ah yes, the bit …' muttered the latter.

I watched as they walked away through the displays. I found myself wondering what their wives looked like.

As for my own wife, I had found nothing to say in response

to her confession. I had taken the news in silence, and she had got up from the sofa, saying she was thirsty. I found her in the kitchen with a glass of mint cordial in her hand. Rain lashed the window.

'What's happened to us?' I asked.

'I don't know,' she said quietly.

I felt no resentment. Her response was sincere. She didn't know, and neither did I. Life had brought us together, and now it was pulling us apart. Was that all our path through life amounted to? We were no more significant than the hundreds of millions of others like us, who had separated before us and would separate after us. It was disappointing indeed to find we were just like all the rest. Just as cowardly, just as small, trotting out our hypocritical statements about Emma, who didn't need to know everything straight away. I pointed out that Emma was no longer a child.

'She's more fragile than you think,' said Sidonie.

And what about me? What about my fragility? Who cared about that? No one. Once again, I was left to do the dirty work on my own. Alone to face my father's death, and my mother's, alone to face the challenges at work, climbing the ladder rung by rung, alone to face the thug on the metro platform, alone to face Louvier, and that charlatan Di Caro. Through every solitary battle, my cigarettes had been my loyal companions. In another life, I would have sat and lit a cigarette. I felt beaten, betrayed, and yet I couldn't hold Sidonie solely responsible for what had happened. I had played my part in the breakdown of our marriage, and I understood how difficult it was for her to have a husband who knew the name of only one painter: Francis Bacon. And that, for all the wrong reasons. All we had done was drink together whenever we met. I had never seriously discussed art with him or anyone else at a private view, and at one such event, I had written a now notorious comment in the visitors' book.

The man I held responsible for everything was the artist whose grinning face appeared on the cover of every American magazine: the carboniser-in-chief. He was the thief in this story. He had entered my lair without my knowing, and stolen away the thing I treasured most. I could see him now, with his arrogant air and scornful smile, at the exhibition of his chargrilled pigeons under their glass domes. 'Why?' he had murmured. 'That is the question.' I'd give that midget genius his answer. In the shape of a tailor-made death. Old Grandpa Edward's recipe for petrol-filled light bulbs would deliver the perfect send-off, it seemed to me. A fitting tribute to the outlandish artworks of Damon Bricker.

The artist was refusing to give anything away about his latest masterpiece, soon to be unveiled at the Paris International Art Fair. So be it. I would silence him once and for all.

I had bought a can of petrol at the garage on the Champs-Élysées and a syringe at the pharmacy. The question of the light bulbs remained to be resolved. What type of bulb did Bricker have at home? Screw or bayonet cap? Globe or flame-shaped? This particular murder differed from Louvier's in its motivation. Sidonie would not be coming back if I eliminated her lover. Nothing would ever be the same again. In a certain sense, I was making my debut as an artist; I would get one over on Bricker. He only burned animals.

Inevitably, while in this quiet interlude, the calm before the storm, I found myself asking where my life had gone. It had slipped through my fingers like sand. My appointment to the top job at HBC was all that remained. As Sidonie had made a point of reminding me. Clearly, she had thought it preferable for us to negotiate this difficult passage at a time when everything was going brilliantly in my career. I would have that at least, she was thinking, though she never said so out loud.

Why was I not still in my first-floor office, smoking my cigarettes? Why was HBC no longer there? Why had Sidonie found 'someone else'? The questions sprang to mind unbidden, and there was no one to offer an answer. We would never go to the beautiful villa on stilts in the Caribbean. I wanted life to stop for a while or to go back in time, right back to the photograph of me as a child in the Tuileries, and to stay there forever. But that was impossible. The dynamics of murder had been set in motion. Just as a quiet smoke had been the most obvious solution to every annoyance, so murder had become my escape in the face of the many obstacles placed in my path. The next time I felt true pleasure in smoking, Damon Bricker would have joined his genial colleague Francis Bacon.

I had found his address by looking in my wife's work diary. My plan was to stop by and talk to him about Sidonie; he owed me that much, and wouldn't refuse. My real aim would be to check the light bulbs in his studio. I had an ulterior motive, too: I wanted to see him alive one last time and try to understand what my wife saw in him.

He lived in a quiet, secluded neighbourhood near the Porte de Bagnolet, in the twentieth arrondissement, the area they call 'la campagne à Paris' – a rustic idyll in the big city. The description was apt. As I walked along the narrow streets, urban Paris receded. Everything here was different – the paving stones, the façades of the houses. This was another Paris, a non-existent Paris, or at least one in a different dimension. The sunlit afternoon added to the curious effect. The silence and the bright light on the white house fronts suggested almost any other town, anywhere in Europe. It came as no particular surprise to me that my wife's lover should inhabit a parallel universe. Wasn't that the role of lovers, to be near and distant all at once, to appear only at the right time, in the right place, and to evaporate as soon as their loved one's everyday life resumed? Passage Boudin was where the great genius had chosen to make his home. Not so much a passage as a short, rather narrow cobbled lane lined with small houses and courtyards of the kind that are often seen on the hillsides overlooking venerable port cities. Was the name a reference to the black pudding or the well-known painter of Normandy beach scenes? I had no idea. I passed a grey cat, which I hoped would never find its way into Bricker's yard if it didn't want to end up under a glass dome. It was sitting on a low wall and made no attempt to slip away as I approached, but watched me with its golden eyes and that strange smile so characteristic of its species. It seemed to be telling me it knew exactly what I was up to, and that it was not in the least bit bothered. My secret was safe.

I reached Bricker's house, and poked my head through a half-open door leading to a small courtyard with a table and two wicker armchairs. 'Sidonie has been here,' I thought immediately. 'Her eyes have surveyed this scene.' Everything I saw now, she had seen before. I was getting to know the place she already knew: at the back of the courtyard, a set of big glass doors opened onto the ground floor of the house. There was one upper floor, with a terrace enclosed in a kind of modern glass conservatory. He had installed his studio in a former artisan's workshop. I walked towards the glass doors. A large rusted sculpture stood in front of them, a tangle of metal that was difficult to identify. The rust trickled away towards a drain cover in the middle of the courtyard. It looked like a trail of dried blood imprinted on the grey stonework.

I slid the glass door across. In the middle of the big room stood a tarnished metal table like the ones I had seen in TV shows, used for dissecting bodies. A vast set of industrial shelves held dozens of jars containing powders and solvents. Large grey plastic storage boxes covered in silver thermal foil were piled up to the ceiling – there were at least twenty. I moved across to the table and found a blackened bird's foot lying on the metal surface. I picked it up and examined it closely. How did Bricker go about his work? I had no idea. The results appeared fossilised and carbonised in equal measure.

'Hello,' said a distinct voice behind me.

I turned round.

Damon Bricker stood framed in the doorway, dressed in dark-grey workman's overalls with a zip up the front.

'Welcome,' he said.

'Don't say that. You don't mean it,' I told him.

He gave a small resigned smile. I took my pack of cigarettes and my lighter out of my pocket.

'Is that a joke?' he asked coldly. 'Have you seen the products I've got stored in here? One cigarette butt not properly extinguished and the whole lot would go up in flames.'

I looked at him and nodded. I was smiling, too, now, though he didn't notice. I put the packet back.

'Have you come to talk about Sidonie?'

The very sound of my wife's name on his lips revolted me. He came towards me. 'If he pats me gently on the shoulder and says, "Sorry, old chum," I'll kill him on the spot,' I thought.

'I've come on my own account. Sidonie doesn't know I'm here,' I said.

'And I won't tell her you've been. I don't want complications, I'm in the middle of working, and I need to concentrate!' he shouted the last words suddenly, very loud, and his voice resonated around the room. 'I'm sorry,' he said after a few seconds of silence. 'But you haven't come at a very good time.'

'Husbands never do,' I said.

But he appeared not to be listening. He pulled a switch connected to a thick cable and the room lit up. I looked up at the source of the sudden light. I hadn't noticed it until now (it was transparent and hung very high up) but suspended from the roof was a gigantic glass chandelier, entwined with a thousand crystalline flowers and leaves.

'It's a genuine Murano,' said Bricker, who must have followed my gaze. 'The very finest eighteenth-century Venetian craftsmanship. Magnificent, isn't it?'

'Magnificent,' I said quietly, for non-aesthetic reasons of my own.

Seven, eight, nine … I counted at least ten light bulbs.

'It lights my workbench,' he said, reaching for a cord.

He ran the cord through its pulley and the chandelier descended very low over the metal table. 'A gift from heaven,' I thought. As if Bricker had orchestrated everything over time to bring about the precise end I had planned for him. If he stood beneath the chandelier when the bulbs exploded, I would create the finest bonfire imaginable. Round, transparent bayonet caps, I noted.

'You really want to talk about Sidonie?'

'Actually, I don't any more,' I said.

I had the information I needed. I could leave. Which is what I was preparing to do when he gave me a curious look and thrust out his chin.

'I'm going to let you in on a secret,' he said, with a conspiratorial smile.

I was expecting to hear about some shameful holiday he had taken in my wife's company, or that their liaison had been going on for longer than I had thought.

'You'll be the only one to know what my project is,' he said earnestly.

He took a papier-mâché model down from a shelf and placed it on the table, sweeping the carbonised bird's foot aside with the back of his hand. He began to tell me all about his *Burning Genesis*, to be unveiled at the Paris International Art Fair. He would be installing large charred animals – ostrich, deer, buffalo, giraffe – in a completely enclosed space measuring three hundred square metres. The viewer would enter the space, and their eyes would have to become accustomed to the dark in order to make out the shapes of the animals, which would be completely covered in glow-worms twice a day. That was what was in the big cases covered in thermal foil piled up to the ceiling: phosphorescent glow-worms that he had been bringing in by the containerload for the past month, for his trial runs, and which were costing him a fortune. The effect would be astounding, and no photographs would be allowed. Each day, the hundredth visitor would leave with a glass jar containing a glow-worm, hermetically sealed, signed and dated. A masterpiece. The resurrection of the body, he said, because the worms symbolised creatures of light, bringers of the hope of an afterlife.

Chargrilled animals, glow-worms, the whole idea was grotesque, and a thousand leagues from the world I inhabited. A headhunter in the business world couldn't compete with that. 'Perfectly sickening,' I had written once, in the visitors' book of an exhibition, and I had no regrets. Artists of Bricker's ilk were swindlers and charlatans, just like Di Caro. Second-rate actors and colourful clowns, playing to the gallery and turning hot air into gold. I had a clear conscience at least. A single minute of my career had more moral value than the millions of dollars generated by a Damon Bricker in his lifetime. Me, I was real, and my work was real, not like these artists and their oeuvre, insubstantial holograms, mirages in the desert of Western culture. I felt no guilt for the crime I was about to commit. Without his nebulous ideas, Damon Bricker was nothing. A trail of smoke dispersing on the air. He didn't exist. He was the opposite of flesh and blood, no more alive than his carbonised animals. My wife was cheating on me with a phantom, a spectre. That was the worst of it. I would have preferred a lifeguard, a male model or even a gigolo to take my place in her affections. But not a Damon Bricker.

His account came to an end at last and he stared at me in silence. False prophet. Pedlar of cheap trinkets.

'Why tell me all this? You should be telling Sidonie, not me,' I said.

'But the reason I can tell you,' he objected, 'is because you won't understand. What I'm saying is like water off a duck's back to you. Don't look at me like that, Monsieur Valantine,' he said as I remained silent. 'You look like an assassin.'

'But I *am* an assassin, Monsieur Bricker,' I replied, with supreme calm.

I turned to leave without saying goodbye. Time to buy those bayonet-cap light bulbs.

Drilling a hole in a light bulb takes skill, dexterity and practice. I had acquired around thirty, hoping to succeed with at least ten. I had installed my makeshift workshop in my lock-up garage, five storeys below ground in the car park under our building. Shut inside, sitting cross-legged in front of my car, I plugged in the Dremel, ready to exercise 'precision control'. The pin-thin carbon-tipped bit turned so fast it all but disappeared. Luckily, I had had the good sense to wear gloves, because the first bulbs shattered in my hands. I felt the lack of a 'Frequently Asked Questions' section on Grandpa Edward's blog: I would happily have left a message to ask how exactly to set about drilling the holes. The tenth attempt was more successful: you had to hold the bulb firmly against your stomach, then drill while barely touching the glass. Once I had worked out the technique, the others were drilled quickly and easily. In less than ten minutes, I had the exact number of light bulbs, pierced in the right place. Using the syringe, I extracted an approximate amount of petrol from the can and injected it into the bulbs. With a small piece of Scotch tape fixed over each hole, the job was complete. The bulbs were one-third full of liquid, their filaments dipped into the petrol. I filled an eleventh bulb, because a trial run was essential. With this in mind, I had bought a bulb socket fitted with two long electric cords and a switch. Once my test light bulb was fitted into place and the cord plugged into the mains, all I needed to do was switch it on and it would explode. All things considered, it would be impossible to try this out in my garage space. My day of DIY had begun on Saturday after lunch, and it would end early that evening in the Bois de Boulogne. I was sure to find a deserted spot in which to test the old hitman's story.

I parked my car at the end of a tree-lined road overlooking the Périphérique, on the Boulogne side. There was no one in sight, and the thin strip of grass down the middle was unlikely to catch fire. The perfect spot. If there was one thing my skills as a handyman extended to, it was recharging car batteries, handling jump leads, unspooling the cables and checking the voltage. I had my electricity supply – less powerful than for an entire building, but enough to light the filament in a bulb. With the bonnet up, I was just setting out what I needed and making ready to place my light bulb on a stone block on the tarmac when a small white van appeared and parked about ten metres away. The heavily made-up blonde at the wheel stared at me through the windscreen. She reversed, killed the engine, seemed to hesitate, then opened the door. Endless legs in high Plexiglas heels, a pink sequinned miniskirt, a black bra supporting an impressive pair of breasts, dyed blond hair in a messy perm. She loped slowly towards me. The closer she came, the stranger and smoother her face looked. Neither young, nor old. A comic-book face. She came to a halt in front of me and smiled.

'Will you be staying long?' she asked politely, in a voice deeper and more masculine than my own.

'No,' I said, somewhat thrown.

'I only ask because I'll be starting work soon. People will be passing through.'

'I'll be gone by then, don't worry.'

Reassured, she nodded and shimmied a little on her high heels.

'Tell me, I hope I'm not intruding …'

She trailed off in mid-sentence.

'Please, Mademoiselle, intrude by all means,' said I, very much the man of the world.

She was clearly pleased that I had called her Mademoiselle.

'Do you have a light? I've come out without mine, silly bitch that I am.'

'A light? ... Yes, I do, here.'

I rummaged in my pockets and held out my Bic lighter. I told her she could keep it.

'You're too sweet,' she said, fishing a cigarette out of her basque.

She lit up and took a drag.

'Have you broken down?'

'Not at all, this is an experiment.'

Her extraordinary shoes tapped along the tarmac. She leaned in to look at the engine, then followed the leads to the light bulb.

'Will it light up?'

'It'll explode,' I told her.

Not wanting to alarm her, I told her straight away that I was a pyrotechnics operator, working in films. After my beginnings as a magician, it was the logical next step.

'Amazing. Can I watch?'

'You certainly can. Stand back.'

We stood to one side, while I gripped the switch.

'Watch out ...' I said, and pressed it.

The bulb shattered in a blaze of flame that shot almost a metre into the air. A second later, a burning puddle of petrol flickered on the tarmac.

'Fantastic!' she gasped.

I smiled, as if we had just completed an impressive trick together.

I tidied everything away, piece by piece, tossed the remains of the socket into a tote bag, then made sure the puddle of petrol was fully extinguished. Perfect. That American grandpa was truly a genius.

'Wait!' she called out to me as I was closing the bonnet and preparing to leave.

She came towards me, taking short, quick steps on her high heels.

'You know what? I like you,' she said, holding out a pink business card with her mobile number on it. 'If ever you feel like a little ... relaxation, I do house calls, too.'

I drove off along the road through the trees and tossed the card out of the window, wondering what 'Maya's' life had been like since her days as a little boy in his classroom at school. His past probably felt even more distant than my afternoon in the Tuileries.

I had used every ruse I could think of to determine which evenings Sidonie would be eating out the following week, and hence her schedule of dates with Bricker. There could be no question of him switching on the chandelier while my wife stood beside him underneath it. The atmosphere between us was not highly charged, contrary to what I had feared. We had barely discussed the subject since our initial conversation. If 'conversation' was indeed the appropriate term for the few words we had exchanged on the stormy afternoon of her confession that we would, very likely, not be growing old together. Emma still hadn't been informed about the new arrangements in her parents' lives. Would it even upset her as much as all that? I had begun to wonder, but I respected Sidonie's wishes: she wanted to tell Emma herself, and that suited me fine.

'Do you love him?' I had asked her one evening in the kitchen.

Sidonie had been slow to reply.

'We have a great many things in common,' she said quietly, at length, without looking at me.

That didn't answer my question, but I refrained from saying so. The conversation might have turned sour, leading to sudden changes of plan that would have left me having to start from scratch: Sidonie might have slammed the door and gone to live with Bricker, for example. I kept to my passive role. Passive in appearance only, of course, because in my head the cogs were turning at full speed, and my cigarette consumption had followed suit. I was almost back to my two packets a day. The one I would savour, the one that would bring heady intoxication, would be the one I'd smoke on Passage Boudin, watching the flames.

Tuesday night. Everything seemed to fall into place. On Tuesday night, Sidonie would be home to have dinner with Emma. I would be at work, and not due back until late. Before dinner, Sidonie would be out at a private view with Damon Bricker. He was behind with his installation for the International Art Fair. In all likelihood, he would head back to his studio to carry on working afterwards. During the private view, his studio would be empty. That was when I would strike.

The day began with a meeting of all the departmental heads, convened by me in the purple room. I wanted to redefine our search strategies for Asia. More and more French executives were prepared to work in the region, lured chiefly by the salaries, double or triple what they could earn at home, and a standard of living far higher than in France. Some posts came with apartments plus a driver and three housekeepers. To match that in Europe, they would need to climb several rungs on the corporate ladder. On which subject, I wondered why our cleaner Maria was still only coming to our apartment twice a week. Since my promotion, we could afford much more. I wrote a note to myself: 'Maria, full-time?' I would have to talk to Sidonie about it one day. I spent almost the entire afternoon in my office, making calls to our high-placed contacts. Lobbying, in the current parlance. 'Schmoozing', as Gold would say. It was an anglicised Yiddish term, he told me, the perfect expression of the gentle smoothing and stroking involved. Schmoozing went a lot further than lobbying. It was all about services rendered with pleasure, and useful friendships to be maintained. I had been schmoozing in my office for several hours when my mobile rang. Five o'clock. I extinguished my twenty-second cigarette in my crystal ashtray. My plan was under way.

I hid on Passage Boudin, behind a low wall. The perfect vantage point for Bricker's house. At 6 p.m. precisely, just as I was beginning to despair, he emerged onto the street. Fashionably late, like any self-respecting celebrity. He wore jeans and a dinner jacket over a white shirt with no tie. He walked past my wall without seeing me. Violent death was becoming the norm for tie-less men, I thought. He turned the corner of the street. I counted one minute, watching the smooth passage of the second hand on my Rolex, then entered his property. The door to the courtyard stood ajar. I passed the wicker furniture for the second time and walked up to the glass doors leading to the studio. I put down my black leather case, packed that morning with ten petrol-filled light bulbs, sealed with Scotch tape and wrapped in Kleenex. From here on, everything would go according to plan. I took out my two keys, copied at the while-you-wait bar in the metro, and inserted the most likely-looking one into the lock. It opened.

My plan for getting into the studio had cost me a good few headaches and numerous packets of aspirin. Unlike old Grandpa Edward, I didn't have the backing of the CIA: no one would come to my aid. How could I get into Bricker's place in his absence? I had decided to use a hammer to break the glass door. The only possible solution, it seemed to me. The broken glass would arouse Bricker's suspicion, for sure, but it wouldn't stop him from switching on his chandelier. This potential grey area in my plan bothered me nonetheless, until one evening I spotted Sidonie's bunch of keys on the chest of drawers in the hallway. There were two new additions:

one in black metal; the other small, flat and gold-coloured. I had taken them to the key bar straight away, before it closed, to make duplicates. The keys could only be to Bricker's place. I was not mistaken.

Entering the studio, I started in shock. A stag lay stretched out atop the big tarnished-steel table. A proper stag from the forest. Its feet were tied together and extended out over the edge. How on earth had that madman Bricker managed to have such a creature delivered? Its very presence seemed an ill omen. After a few seconds, during which I tried to collect myself, I moved forward to examine its head, which hung down over the edge of the table top. The antlers almost touched the floor. I knelt. The animal's eyes were open and its tongue lolled. There was no sign of a bullet wound; the marks were doubtless on the other side of the body. I reached out to touch the antlers, which were covered in a kind of velvety substance, like a brown moss that grew up to the tips before gradually thinning out. If I had lost my nerve then, I think my hands would have begun to shake, such was the suffering and supplication expressed by this animal alone. I operated the pulley. The huge chandelier, already quite low over the table, came down a little further. Carefully, one by one, I removed the light bulbs and replaced them with my own. When the tenth bulb had been fitted, I raised the whole thing by a metre or so, to return it to its original position. I stepped back. Multiplied tenfold, the experiment in the Bois de Boulogne promised a fine conflagration. I bent over the stag's head once again. A tear trickled from its glassy eye. I had to get out of there as fast as possible. It occurred to me that it might not be quite dead, and the very idea made me feel sick.

After locking the door behind me, I walked away down Passage Boudin with Bricker's light bulbs in my case. Sixteen minutes past six. All that remained now was for me to return to my hiding place behind the low wall and wait. Just as I was about to hide, a figure appeared at the end of the lane. A man, walking fast, holding a phone to his ear. The closer he came, the less I could believe my eyes. Still in the same suit, with his hair slicked back and a cigar between his fingers, the man from the café in Abbesses was walking towards me. He drew level with me and raised his eyebrows.

'Well, well. Hello there.' He shook my hand.

What was he doing here? Did he live on Passage Boudin? I was so curious I just had to ask.

'Just a moment,' he said to the person on the other end of the phone. 'No, no,' he told me. 'I've never been here before. What about you? Do you live here?'

'I don't either.'

'How's it going with the cigarettes?'

'OK. And the cigars?'

'Still my poison of choice,' he said, indicating his, as thick as a stair rod. 'Evening!'

And he walked away. Our meeting didn't seem to surprise him in the least. I had shaken his hand, but that meant nothing. At the end of the street, he turned and waved before disappearing suddenly, obscured by the corner of a building. Even now, I have my doubts as to whether he was real.

The long hours spent lying in wait allowed me to become aware of a thousand insignificant sounds, snatches of conversation whose distance from me it was impossible to tell; perhaps they had been carried there on the wind. The rustle of leaves, a few miaows, the clatter of shutters.

The hunt. The word sprang to mind again like an obsession. I was feeling what predators feel as they lurk silently in the undergrowth. I had that extraordinary patience that makes them remain for hours outside the burrow of their prey. The light was slowly fading when I heard the sound of a motorbike. I listened out. The machine drew nearer and stopped with a racket of oiled chains outside Bricker's door. My heart began to beat frantically. Bricker was riding pillion. My head spun. I could not stop this now. If he invited the black-leather-clad biker in for a drink, I would be killing two people at once. I would be responsible for the death of an innocent person.

'OK, *salut*.'

'See you at the pavilion!'

'You'll definitely come?'

'Absolutely, don't worry!'

The motorbike roared away to the far end of the lane. 'Saved,' I thought, taking a deep breath. I heard the courtyard door shut with a creaking of hinges, then Bricker walking towards his studio. Slowly, I reached into my pocket. I hadn't smoked since I'd arrived. The next cigarette would be the most intoxicating of all. I took out my pack and sniffed the cigarettes before tapping one out and putting it in my mouth. I slipped my hand into my other pocket.

Nothing.

With frantic staccato gestures, I patted my trouser pockets. Panic. Nothing. I patted my jacket again. Nothing. No light. 'I don't believe it,' I muttered in panic. I couldn't have made such a stupid mistake. But I had. I had used other lighters since the one I had given to the girl in the woods. I had lighters, lots of them. At home, in the office, everywhere, everywhere except here, except now. As these thoughts assailed me a great explosion rang out along the lane. A flash burst like lightning from behind Bricker's wall and I hurried into the courtyard.

The studio was in flames; the glass doors were lit with a flickering yellow blaze. I stood watching, as if hypnotised, when the door opened. Damon Bricker was on fire. He staggered a few steps, but his movements were uncoordinated and he was emitting a kind of growling noise. This only served to fan the flames. He caught sight of me at last and stood rooted to the spot, open-mouthed. No more sounds rose in his throat. He was burning up, right there; his clothes, his hands, his face and hair. I stood as if turned to stone before this man in flames, whose eyes stared fixedly into mine and who seemed unable to feel the heat of the fire any more. I thought of Sidonie, and this man, who had taken her from me, his ghastly works of art, defiling the animal kingdom. I thought of myself, and my life, going up in smoke as surely as Bricker's studio. Suddenly, he stiffened and became completely motionless, like a waxwork starting to melt. And so I popped the cigarette back in my mouth and stepped forward slowly towards the sizzling creature. I lit the end of my cigarette from the flames devouring his chest. Bricker fell backwards like a broken automaton, and I took a long, slow drag. The most murderous of all. My personal masterpiece. Pure sacrilege. The smoke entered my lungs, and it was as if it penetrated every neural pathway in my brain, every vein in my body, and possessed it entirely. The pleasure was more intense than ever before. I took a seat in the wicker armchair and smoked the cigarette slowly, puff after puff, watching as the glass doors to the studio shattered in the heat.

One man under a metro train, another poisoned by a toxic frog, a third dashed from his balcony rail, a fourth reduced to ashes. I thought then that if I could not reconnect with the pleasure of smoking by other means, I would be unable to stop killing. I had gone too far; there was no way back. The pleasure would land me behind bars. And the man responsible for my 'unskilled repair job', in the words of the porter in the fruit and vegetable section at Rungis, would be waiting for me in the yard of La Santé Prison. He alone could reverse what he had done.

When the police and fire brigade arrived, they found me sitting in the wicker armchair. With a cigarette in my hand.

The smoke expelled from my lungs mingles with the fog of everyone's breath this morning. It's barely two degrees above zero, and at first glance, it seems as if every man in the yard is a smoker. I'm in the only designated smoking area left in Paris. With each cigarette, the euphoria is felt anew. I have lost my liberty, but at least I'm free to smoke. On which subject, the warning on the packets: 'Smoking seriously harms your health' is the butt of frequent jokes in this place.

I lean back against a section of wall in a shaft of sunlight that warms the stone and my face. When I close my eyes, the fine membrane of my eyelids forms a screen that turns wholly red. Orangey-red, with infinite variations.

I lift the cigarette to my lips, inhale, and instinctively open my eyes. Smoking in sunshine with your eyes closed is like smoking in the dark. Very unsettling. You can't see the curls of smoke. You don't feel the pleasure.

I check my apple-green Swatch, an item that incites no jealousy here, bought as a cheap replacement for my Rolex Oyster, which was consigned to the lockers on my way in. Another five minutes and the break will be over. Afterwards, I'll answer my post. Definitely enough time for another. I take a drag and the pale-blue smoke mingles harmoniously with the rays of light and the morning mist. I drop the butt to the ground and crush it with my heel. I put my hand in my jacket and take hold of the gold-coloured pack, from which I remove another cigarette.

'A light, M'sieur Valantine?'

Marc doesn't wait for my answer, but clicks a lighter and holds it up in front of my face. I light the end of my cigarette. The tip glows. First drag. Marc's hair is prematurely white, and even a pure-bred Breton would envy his pale-blue eyes. Marc was born in Courbevoie; he's a likeable man. A friend.

'Thank you, Marc,' I say, with a half-smile, lowering my eyes for a second.

It's a ritual of extreme subtlety, unbeknown to Marc, but which reminds me of the luxurious bars and ultra-private clubs frequented by businessmen in a hurry, the clan to which I once belonged. In such places, the barmen and head waiters light their customers' cigarettes. Lighting another person's cigarette is a gesture of respect and intimacy all at once. A kind of higher understanding. The last spark of a now lost civilisation. The world-champion cigarette lighters were the barmen at Harry's Bar, the famous establishment on the Rue Daunou, where I would stop for a gin from time to time on my way home from work. The customers would thank them with a slight tilt of the head, as I have just thanked Marc. For him, I'm one client among 813 others. A little different, perhaps, because I have earned his trust. At first, he didn't like me at all. He found me solitary and arrogant. But we got to know one another one afternoon, in the yard, while discussing the shape of a passing cloud. Things are simpler in here. Marc isn't supposed to share his private life with the inmates; in fact it's strictly forbidden. But his son had just been hired by a firm of headhunters and he asked me if I had any tips or advice to offer. Distance learning of sorts, through a proxy tutor. I played along. I gave him one or two personal secrets and tactics. They're of no use to me now. The advice soon bore fruit and Marc was grateful. Since then, he lights my cigarettes whenever the occasion presents itself.

He's moving away now, swinging his truncheon behind his back. He exchanges a few words with Giani Sosa, a pleasant mafia boss who smokes Davidoff cigarillos. Fifteen years behind bars for armed robbery and attempted escape. A little further away, Pierre Quimper, our senior inmate, seventy-six years old, packs his pipe and strikes a match in the sunshine. Life for double murder: he's been here for thirty-eight years. Pierre has done some amusing sums, counting up the number of times he's packed his pipe in prison: he makes it a total of 55,480, including leap years.

Leaning against the wall, Di Caro, as well-built as ever, searches the pockets of his yellow tracksuit. His luxuriant beard has turned grey at the chin. I watch him move his lips: he's probably stifling a curse I can't hear. He comes over.

'Got a light? I've left mine in the library.'

'You should give up,' I tell him, lighting his cigarette.

'Very funny,' he mutters, taking his first drag.

When I set foot in the yard for the first time, while I was in custody awaiting trial, I had made straight for Di Caro. The closer I got to him, the more I felt as if I were going back in time. I saw myself in his apartment. I saw the small sitting room, with the sunlight streaming over the parquet floor. The green velvet sofa. I can even remember the smell of fresh paint. He gave a fatalistic smile as I approached.

'Hello,' he said simply, with a slight raising of the eyebrows that seemed to add: 'Quite a lot has happened since our last meeting, wouldn't you say?'

'You smoke. That's rich,' I said. And at my sudden burst of laughter, he lifted his chin with an ironic glance.

'I started in here; there's not much else to do. I'm in for four years.'

'I'll be here a little longer.'

'I know; I've been following your exploits in the newspapers. Impressive.'

The press had seized on my 'exploits', as Di Caro called them. The pundits revelled in my somewhat unusual case. Doctors, psychoanalysts, criminologists and tobaccologists had expounded for months on my case. The national daily *Libération*, well known for its arch headlines, had borrowed the warning from cigarette packets everywhere: 'Smoking Kills'. The words appeared above my photograph, filling the front page. I was smiling, with my head thrown back slightly and a lighted cigarette between my lips, holding my handcuffed wrists below my chin. None of that was my doing: a young man had come up to me on the steps of the police headquarters on Quai des Orfèvres, as I was being taken in under escort. He had held out a cigarette in front of my face. I had seized it between my teeth. A second later, a journalist had clicked his lighter in front of me and I had lit the cigarette and taken a drag as I passed by. The flashbulbs had popped, and one photographer had captured the moment forever. The whole thing was over in a matter of seconds, because the police officers quickly tore the cigarette from my mouth, then forcibly pushed the mob of journalists back. The picture went around the national news networks, fascinating some, horrifying others.

'Will you mention me at your trial?' Di Caro had asked.

'Of course, you have your share of responsibility in all this,' I said.

'As if I wasn't in enough shit already ...' he sighed.

'So we'll do each other a favour. I won't accuse you too heavily, and you can reverse what you did.'

'I'm not really a hypnotist, as you know,' he said, crushing his cigarette under the toe of his trainer.

'One session; you owe me that much, surely?'

'OK, we'll see next time in the yard. But you return the favour.'

'Deal.'

My hypnosis took place, discreetly, in the yard, during a break. Di Caro swore he had learned his technique from a nightclub illusionist who had taught him the vocal trick to make people fall asleep and wake up. That was all he knew. Alternative medical and therapeutic practice had never been part of his armoury. We found a quiet corner by a wall and sat down next to one another as if we were enjoying the sunshine. He gave me the routine about the beach and the grains of sand. This time, I gazed not through a window at the wall opposite, but at a watchtower. I felt myself drift away.

'Try lighting up and tell me if it's worked. I can't guarantee anything,' he said, when I awoke.

He went off to organise an evening of football on TV with Giani Sosa and some other inmates. I clicked my lighter and lit the end of the cigarette. From the first puff, everything flooded back, as if this cigarette was the first of my entire life. I was back in the summer of my *baccalauréat*, in the farmhouse dining room in Normandy, in front of the fire. I could almost taste the Calvados we had drunk during our game of Monopoly.

As the good fairy Nicotine took me in her arms once again, a snatch of that evening's conversation came back to me, echoing in my mind, down the years. It was Marie's voice. The words she had called out while I celebrated my smoker's nuptials, the irresistible chemistry of my first cigarette. I had left the table and she was playing for me. She had made a bad move. 'Fabrice ... Hey, Fabrice! Bad news ... You're in jail!'

That evening, absorbed in the pleasure of smoking, I didn't mind at all about being in jail.

More than thirty years later, nothing had changed.

The pleasure had returned. For life.